RATBAGS AND RASCALS

When some rascals kidnap Clarissa, they begin to think she must be the biggest ratbag of them *all! All* she ever does is bully them . . .

And Lindy finds life with Parker-Hamilton, the perfect household robot, isn't much fun either. He's such a rascal, he only allows folk to watch television for an hour a day and gives them a computer schedule of when they are allowed in the living room! They'll have to sort him out . . .

Ratbags and rascals come in all shapes and sizes and all sorts of them can be found in these funny stories by Robin Klein. Good stories to read to yourself or to any ratbags and rascals you might happen to know . . . !

Robin Klein is the author of THE BROOMSTICK ACADEMY which is also published by Hippo Books.

RATBAGS AND RASCALS

Funny Stories
by Robin Klein

illustrated by
Alison Lester

Hippo Books
Scholastic Publications Limited
London

Scholastic Publications Ltd.,
10 Earlham Street, London WC2H 9RX, UK

Scholastic Inc.,
730 Broadway, New York, NY 10003, USA

Scholastic Tab Publications Ltd.,
123 Newkirk Road, Richmond Hill,
Ontario L4C 3G5, Canada

Ashton Scholastic Pty. Ltd.,
PO Box 579, Gosford, New South Wales,
Australia

Ashton Scholastic Ltd.,
165 Marua Road, Panmure, Auckland 6,
New Zealand

First published by J M Dent Pty. Limited, Australia
and produced by P.I.X.E.L. Publishing, Australia

Published in paperback by Scholastic Publications Ltd.,
1987, UK

ISBN 0 590 70622 5

Typeset in Plantin by AKM Associates (UK) Ltd,
Ajmal House, Hayes Road, Southall, London.
Made and printed by Cox and Wyman, Reading, Berks

Contents

The kidnapping
of Clarissa Montgomery

"YOU'LL ONLY HAVE to stay here till your rich guardian pays the ransom," said the kidnapper, whose name was Humphrey. He felt rather sorry for poor little Clarissa. She hadn't said anything since they'd grabbed her from the luxurious grounds of her mansion that afternoon. "I think the poor little kid's in shock," Humphrey said worriedly to Spud, who had masterminded the abduction. Spud didn't care if she was in shock, neither did Milligan.

"Just sit tight and don't cause any trouble, kid," Spud snarled. "Soon as the old man pays the fifty thousand, you'll be sent back."

Clarissa finally spoke. "Fifty thousand?" she said.

"I'm sure he'll manage to find it," said kind-hearted Humphrey reassuringly. "You'll be out of here in no time."

Clarissa looked at him coldly. "You're all mad," she said. "You could have got a whole lot more than fifty thousand. My guardian is loaded."

"She's in shock," Humphrey thought, and made her a cup of cocoa with his own hands.

He'd fixed up a corner of the barn quite nicely with a toffee apple in a saucer. He was fond of little kids.

Spud was setting up a poker game. Clarissa watched silently.

"You don't have to be scared of those gorillas," Humphrey whispered. "They're really harmless."

"I'm not scared of anything," Clarissa said, and drew closer to the table.

"Beat it," growled Spud, but Clarissa looked at his cards, then went round the table and inspected Humphrey's and Milligan's. "Get rid of the red queen and keep the clubs," she said to Humphrey, and he did, and won.

"Scat, kid," said Spud, but Clarissa sat down at the table.

"I want to play, too," she said.

"Go back to your cocoa," Spud ordered, but Clarissa opened her mouth and let out a high-pitched wailing yell. It went on and on, un-bearable in the galvanized-iron roofed barn, and Spud, Milligan and Humphrey covered their ears.

"Maybe she'll stop if we let her play," suggested Humphrey, and dealt out a hand to Clarissa. She stopped screeching and picked up her cards. Then she proceeded, without any trouble at all, to win ten games and fifty pounds.

"It's not very nice, if you ask me," Spud said disgustedly. "Little girls shouldn't know how to cheat at poker."

Clarissa pocketed her winnings and went to bed. She slept very well. In the morning she woke up early. Humphrey, Spud and Milligan were dozing fitfully in uncomfortable chairs. Clarissa made herself a substantial breakfast, then examined the barn.

"Get away from that door!" Spud said, waking up.

"I've seen play forts in council parks better defended than this old barn," Clarissa scoffed. "The police could have this place surrounded and you wouldn't even know. No wonder you only asked for fifty thousand. It's all you're worth."

Spud was so indignant that he bit his pre-breakfast cigar in two. "What became of all the food?" he demanded angrily.

"I had it for my breakfast, of course," Clarissa said.

So Humphrey, Spud and Milligan had to make do with discussing the plans for collecting the ransom money instead. Clarissa listened. "It won't work," she jeered. "Just how do you expect Humphrey to reach the hollow tree in the park past a whole lot of detectives all lying in wait? It's too corny, collecting ransom money from a hollow tree."

"And what would you suggest then, Miss Smarty?" Spud asked.

"Some place where they can't set up an ambush, of course. Tell them to put the money in a briefcase in a plastic bag and drop it off the pier. One of you could get it wearing scuba gear. It's a much better plan than your old hollow tree. I'll draft a new anonymous letter to my rich guardian." Clarissa began cutting letters from Spud's newspaper, even though he hadn't read the racing page yet. She pasted the letters to a sheet of paper, and even Spud had to admit that it looked much more professional than theirs. And she'd doubled the ransom money, too.

"But none of us can scuba dive," Humphrey pointed out.

"I can," said Clarissa crushingly. "I'll collect the money. But only if you give me a share."

"That's only right," said Humphrey. "If she picks it up, she should be given something."

"Ninety-five per cent," said Clarissa. "Or I won't go at all. Anyhow, you wouldn't have any ransom money in the first place, if it wasn't for me."

"If it wasn't for you, we wouldn't be sitting in this draughty old barn with nothing to eat for breakfast

PuT £100,000) IN plasTiC bAG

and dROP off Pier at

nOON toDay Or ELse !

but a toffee apple," said Spud. "I wish we'd concentrated on stealing your rich guardian's valuable oil paintings instead."

"You'd never get near them. They're fitted with electronic alarms."

"I stole the Mona Lisa once," Spud said boastfully.

"And you only got as far as the front door before they caught you. I read about it in the papers. The only way you could steal my guardian's paintings is if I came along and showed you the secret panel where you can cut off the alarm circuit. So there."

Spud sourly began a round of poker while Humphrey went out to deliver the ransom note. Clarissa won another ten games. Spud thought with pleasure that after tonight they'd be rid of her. "Soon as we pick up that briefcase, we'll drop you off at your mansion," he said.

"First we'll come back here and count the money," contradicted Clarissa. "Don't you know you can't trust anyone? You're the most hopeless gang leader I ever met. And you'll have to make plans about leaving the country, too. You'll need to learn a foreign language, but that's no problem. This afternoon you can all study French verbs. I'll supervise. That's after you clean up the getaway car. I'm not going anywhere to pick up ransom money in a car as dirty as that."

She nagged so much that Spud, Humphrey and Milligan went out in the cold and cleaned the car. Clarissa sat at the window and made sure they did a thorough job. Spud, Milligan and Humphrey consoled themselves with thinking of all the goodies they'd buy once they got their hands on the ransom money. "A farm in France," Spud said. "I always wanted one of those."

"I bet you don't know anything about farming, or France," said Clarissa. "It might be a good idea if I came along to advise you. I always give my guardian advice on real estate and money investment and I practically run his affairs for him. I don't know what he'd do without me."

Milligan, Spud and even Humphrey eyed her with distaste. They were getting fed up with the draughty barn, the waiting and the French verbs, and most of all they were fed up with Clarissa and her organizing.

It was almost a relief when the time came to collect the ransom money. They drove to the waterfront, and Clarissa put on the scuba suit and galloped confidently into the sea.

"She might swim to the pier and just pop up and give the alarm," said Humphrey nervously. "Let's get out of here."

"Not without our share of the money," said Spud. "I haven't put up with that kid all day for nothing."

"We won't have to put up with her much longer," said Milligan thankfully. "Soon as we sort out the ransom money, we can drop her off at her mansion, and good riddance. Then it's off to the south of France for us."

"That guardian's welcome to her," said Spud. "We should give the poor old fellow a few thousand pounds back. I feel sorry for him, having to put up with her till she's grown up and married."

"No one would marry her," said Milligan with conviction. "Not even if they were bribed with all of the Montgomery fortune."

They watched the water anxiously, but no police boat bristling with armed constables skimmed into sight. And after fifteen minutes,

Clarissa emerged, carrying a weighted briefcase in a plastic bag. Milligan, Spud and Humphrey tried to grab it from her, but Clarissa put it in the getaway car and sat on it. "Don't be so greedy," she said. "You're making as much noise as kids in a sandpit. You'll just have to wait till we get back to the barn."

On the way back the three gangsters were quite civil to Clarissa. They were all thinking that very soon they could drop her off at her mansion and never have to listen to her again or be ordered about.

Spud had the first try at the locked briefcase, and failed. Milligan failed, too, and then Humphrey had a turn, with his skilful hands that had foiled every bank safe in town. But even he couldn't get the combination lock open.

"What a lot of butterfingers!" said Clarissa, and turned the little numbered cylinder and the lid flew open.

But the briefcase wasn't full of bank notes at all. There wasn't anything but the bricks that had served to weight it down in the water. And one short typed note. Spud snatched it up and read it aloud, and his eyes rounded with horror and disbelief.

DO NOT WANT CLARISSA BACK, SHE IS TOO IRRITATING AND BOSSY. YOU CAN KEEP HER. GLAD TO GET RID OF HER, REGARDS, ALGERNON MONTGOMERY, MILLIONAIRE.

All the kidnappers turned pale and sat down.

"Why are you all sitting down wasting time?" Clarissa demanded, frowning. "We have an oil painting job to plan. And now that I'm in charge of this gang, I expect much better work from all of you."

Hey, Danny!

"RIGHT," SAID DANNY'S mother sternly. "That school bag cost ten pounds. You can just save up your pocket money to buy another one. How could you possibly lose a big school bag, anyhow?"

"Dunno," said Danny. "I just bunged in some empty bottles to take back to the milkbar, and I was sort of swinging it round by the handles coming home, and it sort of fell over that culvert thing down on to a lorry on the motorway."

"And you forgot to write your name and phone number in it as I told you to," said Mrs Hillerey. "Well, you'll just have to use my blue weekend bag till you save up enough pocket money to replace the old one. And no arguments!"

Danny went and got the blue bag from the hall cupboard and looked at it.

The bag was not just blue; it was a vivid, clear, electric blue, like a flash of lightning. The regulation colour for schoolbags at his school was a khaki-olive-brown, inside and out, which didn't show stains from when your can of Coke leaked, or when you left your salami sandwiches uneaten and forgot about them for a month.

"I can't take this bag to school," said Danny. "Not one this colour. Can't I take my books and stuff in one of those green plastic rubbish bags?"

"Certainly not!" said Mrs Hillerey.

On Monday at the bus stop, the kids all stared at the blue bag.

"Hey," said Jim, who was supposed to be his mate. "That looks like one of those bags girls take to ballet classes."

"Hey, Danny, you got one of those frilly dresses in there?" asked Spike.

"Aw, belt up, can't you?" said Danny miserably. On the bus the stirring increased as more and more kids got on. It was a very long trip for Danny. It actually took only twenty minutes – when you had an ordinary brown schoolbag and not a great hunk of sky to carry round with you. Every time anyone spoke to him they called him "Little Boy Blue".

"It matches his lovely blue eyes," said one kid.

"Maybe he's got a little blue trike with training wheels too," said another kid.

"Hey, Danny, why didn't you wear some nice blue ribbons in your hair?"

When Danny got off the bus he made a dash for his classroom and shoved the bag under his desk. First period they had Miss Reynolds, and when she was marking the register she looked along the aisle and saw Danny's bag and said, "That's a very elegant bag you have there, Danny."

Everyone else looked around and saw the blue bag and began carrying on. Danny kept a dignified silence, and after five minutes Miss Reynolds made them stop singing "A Life on the Ocean Waves". But all through Maths and English, heads kept turning round to grin at Danny and his radiantly blue bag.

At morning recess he sneaked into the art room and mixed poster paints into a shade of khaki-olive-brown which he rubbed over his bag with his hankie. When the bell rang he had a grey handkerchief, but the bag was still a clear and innocent blue. "Darn thing," Danny muttered in disgust. "Must be made of some kind of special waterproof atomic material. Nothing sticks to it."

"What are you doing in the art room, Daniel?" asked Miss Reynolds. "And what is that terrible painty mess?"

"I was just painting a Zodiac sign on my bag," said Danny.

"I wish you boys wouldn't write things all over your good school bags. Clean up that mess,

Danny, and go to your next class."

But Danny said he was feeling sick and could he please lie down in the sick bay for a while. He sneaked his blue bag in with him, and found the key to the first-aid box and looked inside for something that would turn bright blue bags brown. There was a little bottle of brown lotion, so Danny tipped the whole lot on to cotton wool and scrubbed it into the surface of the bag. But the lotion just ran off the bag and went all over his hands and the bench top in the sick bay.

"Danny Hillerey!" said the school secretary. "You know very well that no student is allowed to unlock the first-aid box. What on earth are you doing?"

"Sorry," said Danny. "Just looking for some liver salts."

"I think you'd better sit quietly out in the fresh air if you feel sick," Mrs Adams said suspiciously. "And who owns that peculiar-looking blue bag?"

"It belongs in the sport equipment shed," said Danny. "It's got measuring tapes and stuff in it. Blue's our house colour."

He went and sat outside with the bag shoved under the seat and looked at it and despaired. Kids from his class started going down to the oval for sport, and someone called out "It's a beautiful blue, but it hasn't a hood".

Danny glared and said "Get lost" and "Drop dead". Then Miss Reynolds came along and made him go down to the oval with the others.

On the way there Danny sloshed the blue bag in a puddle of mud — but nothing happened, the blue became shinier if anything. He also tried grass stains under the sprinkler, which had the same effect. Amongst the line-up of khaki-olive-brown bags, his blue one was as conspicuous as a Clydesdale horse in a herd of small ponies.

"Hey, Danny, what time's your tap dancing lesson?" said the kids.

"Hey, Danny, where did you get that knitting bag? I want to buy one for my Aunty."

"Hey, Danny, when did you join the Bluebell marching girls' squad?"

Finally Danny had had enough.

"This bag's very valuable if you want to know," he said.

"Rubbish," everyone scoffed. "It's just an ordinary old vinyl bag."

"I had to beg my Mum to let me bring that bag to school," said Danny. "It took some doing, I can tell you. Usually she won't let it out of the house."

"Why?" demanded everyone. "What's so special about it?"

Danny grabbed back his bag and wiped off the traces of mud and poster paint and brown lotion and grass stains. The bag was stained inside where all that had seeped in through the seams and the zipper, and it would take some explaining when his mother noticed it. (Which she would, next time she went to spend the weekend at Grandma's.) There was her name inside, E. Hillerey, in big neat letters. E for Enid.

"Well," said Danny, "that bag belonged to . . . well, if you really want to know, it went along on that expedition up Mount Everest."

Everyone jeered.

"It did so," said Danny. "Look, Sir Edmund Hillary, there's his name printed right there inside. And there's a reason it's this funny colour. So it wouldn't get lost in the snow. It was the bag Sir Edmund Hillary carried that flag in they stuck up on top of Mount Everest. But I'm not going to bring it to school any more if all you can do is poke fun at the colour."

Everyone went all quiet and respectful.

"Gee," said Jeff in an awed voice, and he touched the letters that Danny's mother had written with a laundry marking pencil.

"Gosh," said Mark. "We never knew you were related to that Sir Edmund Hillary."

Danny looked modest. "We're only distantly related," he admitted. "He's my Dad's second cousin."

"Hey, Danny, can I hold it on the bus? I'll be really careful with it."

"Hey, Danny, can I have a turn when you bring it to school tomorrow?"

"I'll charge you ten pence a go," said Danny. "That's fair, for a bag that went up to the top of Mount Everest."

"Ten pence a kid," he calculated. "One hundred kids at ten pence a turn, ten pounds. A new brown school bag. And with a bit of luck, I'll earn all that before someone checks up in the library and finds out Sir Edmund Hillary's name's spelled differently!"

The visitor
(extra-terrestrial)

LINDY DAWSON FOUND the angel when she was helping her dad in the garden. It was half buried in autumn leaves and its poor wings were matted with oil. It had beautiful eyes the colour of a midsummer sky, and hair the colour of pollen under yellow cellophane.

"That one's got problems, with its wings in that state," said Mr Dawson.

They took the angel inside and Mrs Dawson was very impressed to think that they had a visitor like that. The angel was so breathtakingly beautiful that they all gazed, awestruck. The only thing amiss was its wings.

"There's some solvent down in the toolshed, but it's a job that will take weeks," Mr Dawson said. "Each of those little feathers will have to be done separately."

"I don't mind how long it takes," said Mrs Dawson. "No one in this street ever had an angel staying with them before."

For dinner she made a completely white meal, creamed chicken, potatoes in white sauce, and vanilla blancmange. "It doesn't seem proper to serve up things like curried sausages to an angel," she whispered to Lindy.

The angel had beautiful table manners and it didn't leave the table until Mrs Dawson said it could. "I just hope some of those nice manners will rub off on you, Lindy," Mrs Dawson said. The angel didn't sprawl all over the carpet where people couldn't get past, but sat neatly on the couch, with its little gold sandals tucked out of the way, and its hands folded tidily over its gold harp. When all the neighbours came in to look, it stood up and bowed to each of them, and even to the cat.

Then it played its harp. The music was exquisite, though Lindy privately thought that it went on for a bit too long. When everyone clapped, the angel didn't look conceited, but kept its eyes modestly lowered.

Every day Mr Dawson worked at getting the oil out of the angel's feathers. He felt nervous about taking the liberty of touching an angel, even if it was only with cotton wool soaked in solvent. "I feel as though I should put on plastic gloves," he said. But the angel gave him a smile of such rare beauty that he went out and bought an expensive pure white lambswool rug. It didn't seem suitable for someone so exalted to stand on the rather tatty living-room carpet while having its wings repaired.

The angel was very little trouble as a guest. Lindy wondered in amazement how anyone could stay so clean and tidy. Its nails never got dirty, its hair was always as smooth as scented water, and its robe hung in graceful folds and never got creased.

Everyone put on their best manners. Mrs

Dawson was very strict about allowing only wholesome TV programmes while the angel was there, and the family's viewing dwindled to practically nothing as a result. Mr Dawson thought he'd better not do his football pools in the living room, either, or smoke his pipe. He took up stained glass leadlighting instead, though he didn't find that as interesting.

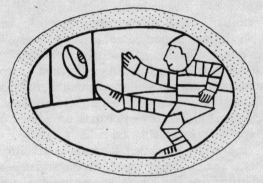

Every time Lindy grizzled about the washing up, Mrs Dawson would say in a shocked voice, "Lindy, what if the angel hears you carrying on like that!" The Dawsons became famous because of the angel, and had their pictures in the papers. Lindy found that teachers at school would say when she did something naughty, "Lindy Dawson! That's not a nice way to behave for a person who has an angel staying at their place!"

Lindy didn't say what she really thought, that she wished the angel had chosen some place else.

Mrs Dawson grew very particular about what the family wore. There was no more slopping around casually in flip-flops, jeans or T-shirts with pictures of pop stars on the front, and no more heated up pizza casually eaten on everyone's knees while they watched "Sale of the Century". Not that the angel ever looked down its splendid nose critically at the way their household was run, but its very presence made everyone strive for perfection. It was so perfect itself in every way.

Lindy looked at its wings jealously and wished she had a pair. It would be marvellous to have wings like that, she thought. You could get into the grand final without paying, and win the hurdles in the school sports easily. But she didn't say anything so disrespectful to the angel. "It must be lovely to be able to sit on clouds and play harp music," she said politely instead.

One night the angel gave its usual after-dinner harp concert, and Mrs Dawson was horrified to find herself yawning half-way through. She turned the yawn into what she hoped looked like a smile of bliss, but decided secretly that she really liked Country and Western music better.

The Dawsons all went to bed early, because they felt they should keep respectable hours while the angel was their guest. They didn't even fight over whose turn it was to put out the dustbin. Lindy would have liked to play her new record, which was called "Kaleidoscope POW!" but she knew it wasn't serious, proper music.

Mr Dawson would have liked to stay up to watch "The Meanest Gun In The West" but knew that would be too frivolous.

Mrs Dawson would have liked to ring her friends to plan the Ladies' Auxiliary Bingo Night, but didn't think it was fitting with the angel in the house.

They went soberly to bed instead, taking sensible books to read, but they didn't read for very long. They were all too tired from the strain of being on such good behaviour for the past few weeks.

In the morning the angel was gone.

"It must have finished cleaning up the rest of the oil itself," said Mr Dawson, bewildered.

"Perhaps it didn't care to stay because we didn't measure up," said Mrs Dawson miserably. "We must have done something to offend it."

"It left a goodbye note," said Lindy.

The note wasn't just an ordinary one written with a biro on a scrap of paper. It was inscribed on fine parchment with gold letters written with a quill, like a page from a mediaeval book. The angel thanked them for repairing its wings so nicely and said what a pleasure it had been staying in such a well-behaved, admirable, perfect household.

"Well, we didn't do anything to offend it," said Mrs Dawson, putting the note up on the mantel. "That's a lovely note." She was thinking, however, that she would just pop down the street and get a nice big Hawaiian Delight pizza for dinner.

"We'll miss that angel," said Mr Dawson. "It was a very good influence." But he was hunting behind the couch cushions for his football pool cards.

Lindy looked carefully at the parchment thank-you note before putting on her "Kaleidoscope POW" record.

The angel certainly did have beautiful writing, and had made only one mistake, which was crossed out neatly. The crossed-out words came between "perfect" and "household".

Lindy, peering at it, was almost certain the words were "UTTERLY BORING".

Parker-Hamilton

MR AND MRS BROWN and Jacqueline thought their new robot was terrific. Only Grandma wasn't very impressed. "Ridiculous-looking thing, if you ask me," she said, with her nose in the air.

"It's going to be worth every dollar," Mrs Brown contradicted. She pressed the robot's starter button and said, giggling a little, "We'd like afternoon tea, please." The robot glided on soundless wheels to the kitchen.

"It's creepy, that's what," said Grandma. "It'd better not break any of my rose pattern china, either."

"That robot has a hundred per cent efficiency guarantee," said Mr Brown. The new robot served an excellent cup of tea and also baked some beautifully light scones.

"We ought to give it a name," said Jacqueline, reading the manual. "You have to feed in a selection of names, and it chooses the one it likes best." The Browns thought of various names and wrote them down on pieces of paper and placed them in the robot's input slot. But all the names were firmly rejected.

"Well, it's one of the more expensive models," said Mrs Brown. "I suppose it's inclined to be a bit fussy."

"It's just plain stuck-up," said Grandma. Mrs Brown wrote down stuck-up names such as Montague and Forsythe, and when she wrote down Parker-Hamilton with a hyphen, the robot flashed a green light.

The Browns had a wonderful time watching Parker-Hamilton do jobs. Mr Brown's business account books were perfectly balanced with no effort on his part. Mrs Brown had the front door repainted and a manicure. Jacqueline's room looked tidy for the first time in years. Parker-Hamilton noiselessly removed the shoes and dumped jeans from under her bed, sorted out her records and repaired all the torn posters on her walls.

Grandma was the only one who didn't hang round admiring the new robot. "I never did like any machine except television," she said stubbornly.

"Parker-Hamilton could finish that bedspread you're crocheting," Jacqueline suggested. She pushed the crochet pattern into the slot, and Parker-Hamilton whirred softly and slid out a perfect square of crochet in six seconds. The square of crochet was even sealed into a small hygienic plastic bag.

Grandma didn't look very grateful. She snatched back her crochet pattern and pushed the wool bag behind the couch. "I'm not staying in the house with that interfering know-it-all," she said crossly. "I'll go to a motel." The robot helpfully packed her suitcase and dialled a taxi.

That night it cooked and served a wholesome, well-balanced, three-course meal. It passed the salt and pepper and even played some very nice violin dinner music. At the end of the meal it brought warm water and towels and washed everyone's hands". Oh, how cute!" said Mrs Brown.

Parker-Hamilton switched on the television in the living room and then went and did the washing up. At ten it went around the house and turned down everyone's bed. It took out the rubbish and locked the front door. Then it hovered in the hallway, humming quietly to itself, with its metal arms folded. Its panel of little lights flickered down to a soft glow.

"That's sweet," said Jacqueline. "It's put itself to sleep for the night."

Mrs Brown had plenty of spare time from then on. She phoned Grandma at the motel and announced triumphantly that she was thinking of taking up opera singing lessons now, because she had so much leisure. But Grandma only snorted and hung up in her ear.

The Brown household routine became dazzlingly efficient. Jacqueline had a pair of clean socks for school every morning without fail. And if she left a wad of used bubble gum on her desk or the bathroom basin, the robot removed it immediately. Jacqueline began to think that it followed her around on purpose because of the bubble gum, and it made her feel self-conscious.

"Everything certainly is well run around here," Mrs Brown said, but she began to sound a little uncertain. Actually, the robot was becoming fiercely possessive about the house-

work. It hated to see newspapers left lying around, and it hovered by Mr Brown when he smoked his pipe, with an ashtray at the ready. "Parker-Hamilton is getting a bit bossy," said Mrs Brown. "Do you know it washed the kitchen floor eighteen times today and then it locked the door and wouldn't let me in there to get a glass of water! Can't you adjust its mechanism, Roger, and tone it down a little?"

Mr Brown studied the manual. "It certainly does need adjusting," said Jacqueline. "I'm not allowed to sit on my bed once it's made. Parker-Hamilton makes this scary buzzing noise."

"I'm afraid this particular model can't be toned down," said Mr Brown. "It's designed to work at peak efficiency."

"How clever," said Mrs Brown, but she sounded a little annoyed. The house was so clean that the curtains hung like sheets of glass and every carpet fibre could be counted. All the books were arranged in perfect grading of size and each one was sealed in a hygienic plastic bag. Everything was so bright and shimmering that the Browns had to wear sunglasses.

Parker-Hamilton didn't like them strolling around the shiny house. It pushed them firmly into the kitchen and showed them a sheet of computer paper with printed instructions. It was a schedule of the times they were permitted to enter the living room.

"This is ridiculous," said Mr Brown. "We're only allowed in the living room to watch TV for one hour each day, and even then we have to wear plastic bags over our shoes. And it says we have to shampoo our hair out at the garden tap because it won't have the bathroom basin used."

They sat down to an uneasy meal. Parker-Hamilton was beginning to be very high-handed about table manners. It rapped Jacqueline over the knuckles for spilling soup on the tablecloth and took away her dessert. Jacqueline burst into tears. "I don't like it any more," she cried. "It's nothing but a big bully!"

Mr Brown worriedly studied the manual again. "There's hundreds of pounds worth of electronic engineering behind that panel, and it's all been designed to produce a perfect household robot," he said. "There's no dial I can alter."

Grandma came in with her suitcase. "I only

came home because I didn't like the marmalade at the motel," she said. "I see you still have that contraption."

The robot quickly whished Grandma's suitcase away and unpacked it. Then it cleared away the meal dishes, and put the chairs in perfect alignment. Then it took all the Browns into the bathroom and they had their teeth cleaned for four minutes each. Parker-Hamilton put plastic bags over their shoes, and they were allowed to go into the living room.

They all looked terribly self-conscious and didn't meet Grandma's eyes. "Why are we watching this boring programme about diesel engines?" Grandma asked.

"Parker-Hamilton chooses each night," said Mrs Brown miserably. "It likes films about engines and motors. It gets annoyed if we change over channels."

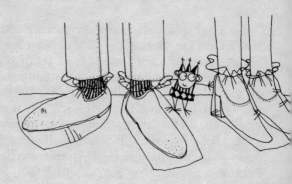

"I always watch the race reviews on a Sunday evening," said Grandma." And where's my crochet?"

"Parker-Hamilton finished it off," said Jacqueline, taking a bundle from the cupboard. It was Grandma's bedspread, completely finished, down to the last six hundred and fortieth tiny perfect square. It was sealed into a plastic bag. "Parker-Hamilton doesn't like unfinished work left lying about," said Jacqueline.

Grandma stared at her rug indignantly. "Years and years of work I'd done on that rug!" she yelled. "And it was good for another fifteen years yet! Now that nosey-parker's gone and ruined all the pleasure!"

"We certainly didn't bargain for it taking over the house like this," said Mr Brown.

"Send it back to the factory," snapped Grandma.

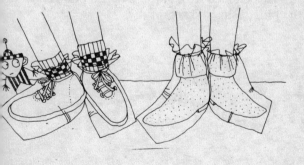

"They don't accept models back," said Mr Brown sheepishly. "I've already telephoned."

Parker-Hamilton's lights blinked and he made a buzzing hornet sound. "It means we have to be quiet while this documentary's on," said Mrs Brown. But Grandma turned the television to her race programme. Parker-Hamilton buzzed rapidly and more loudly.

"Don't you dare speak to me like that!" Grandma ordered. The high-pitched buzzing suddenly stopped. All the angry flashing little lights snapped off, and the robot stood quietly in the middle of the room with its metal arms folded. "That's better," said Grandma. She sat down and began to unravel the crochet rug. Mrs Brown and Mr Brown and Jacqueline all stared at her.

"What happened?" they demanded. "How did you do that?"

Grandma held up the end of an electric flex. "I just switched it off at the wall and pulled out the plug," she said scornfully.

When Alice Jones
got her dress burned

"TELL US ABOUT Alice Jones getting her dress burned, Grandma."

"Oh, you don't want to hear that old story again," said Grandma, but the children insisted. Grandma finished a row of knitting and told them.

"Alice Jones was a girl in my class and she always had nicer dresses than anyone else. She used to show off dreadfully about them. But dresses were dresses in those days." Grandma looked rather severely at the assortment of denim jeans and T-shirts around her. "This particular dress of Alice Jones had a skirt with a frill, and long frilled sleeves, and a high collar, and that had a frill round it, too."

"And it was made of cream material with a pattern of violets and little green leaves!" the children chorused.

"Who's telling this?" Grandma asked testily, and the children shut up and listened. "Well then, Alice Jones boasted for days about her new dress. You couldn't just walk into a store and buy clothes, then. They were made on treadle sewing machines, and we used to look after our clothes properly." Grandma glanced even more severely at a rip in one of the T-shirts and at the frayed hems of a pair of jeans. "When her mother finished the dress, Alice pestered to be allowed to wear it to school. She was supposed to save it for the Sunday School concert, but she was very spoiled and often got her own way."

"So she wore it to school and all the other girls pretended it wasn't anything so special," the children chorused. "But they were sick with jealous fury, really."

"Who's telling this story?" Grandma demanded, and they all fell silent. "Alice Jones wore that dress to school, and we all pretended it wasn't anything special. My friend Louisa said it made Alice Jones look fat, and my sister Lizzie said it made her skin look sallow. But we were all sick with jealous fury, really. Alice Jones swished round school all day in that dress. And the material was lovely, a pattern of violets and green leaves. After school we walked down to the sand dunes."

"And there was a campfire still smouldering."

"Probably lit by a swagman," Grandma said. "They'd come to the farms looking for work. The ashes were still glowing and we added bark and twigs and made a nice little fire. It was chilly in the sand dunes."

"Why was that Alice Jones wearing a flower dress in winter?"

"Because she was very spoiled and vain. Anyhow, she had a flannel petticoat underneath. We sat round the fire and practised singing for the Sunday School concert. And when we got up to go home, Louisa said, 'How funny, the swagman who camped here must have had a shirt exactly the same pattern as Alice Jones's dress!' She held up a big piece of material patterned in violets and green leaves. Alice Jones looked very humiliated to think that a swagman would have a shirt made of the same material as her new dress, and I'm afraid we all crowed about it, and asked her if she had an uncle or a cousin who was a swagman. She got very huffy, because her father owned the store and they were very respectable, and her mother taught at the Sunday School. She said she wouldn't speak to us any more, and turned her back."

"And you all yelled, 'Oh, Alice Jones, wait!' " the children cried.

"No, we didn't. Who's telling this story? Lizzie grabbed her by the arm and just pointed. The back skirt of Alice Jones's new dress had been burned away by the campfire and Alice Jones began to cry." Grandma added rather smugly, "Children were expected to look after their clothes in those days. Material was expensive, not to mention button-holes having to be done by hand, and no washing machines either, or dry-cleaning shops. We rallied round and rubbed away the charred edges of the burned cloth and tried to pin it back, but it was too small. Louisa tried to comfort Alice Jones. Louisa was a very good-hearted girl, and she said she would let Alice borrow her gold bangle to wear to the Sunday School concert. We walked behind Alice so nobody could see her petticoat, which would have been shameful.

OOM AAH

And Alice Jones cried all the way home."

"She sounds a big dill," one of the children muttered.

"Well, she had reason. Her mother had been working on that dress for two weeks."

"Did she get smacked?" one of the children asked hopefully.

"No. She managed to sneak inside and hide the dress in her room. And next day, which was Sunday, we cut off a length of the same material from the roll in Mr Jones's store and worked secretly all that day. We unpicked the skirt of Alice's new dress and put in another section, and sewed it all back together again."

"With the door locked, so her mother couldn't come in and catch you."

"You weren't there. I'm the one telling this story. Mrs Jones was busy at the church hall getting ready for the Sunday School concert."

"Was Alice Jones grateful and nice after that?"

"Only with a little bit of blackmail. My sister Lizzie kept that charred piece of material, and every time Alice Jones was nasty to us at school, and said she wouldn't ask us to her birthday party, Lizzie would say, 'Oh, I must give your mother back that piece of material.' And I don't want to tell that story one more time, so you needn't bother to nag and pester."

But the next day one of the children was ill in bed with measles, and when Grandma brought lunch on a tray, that child said, "Grandma, tell me about the time when Alice Jones got her dress burned."

Plover and Cuff

"A SPACESHIP JUST landed behind our back fence!" Rob told his busy Dad.

"I can't come and look at anything right now," his dad growled.

Rob's mother was ironing some curtains.

"There's a UFO behind our back fence!" Rob said.

"I think these curtains have shrunk a bit in the wash," she said vaguely.

Nobody was interested in the UFO. Rob's brother and sister were playing Monopoly and they pulled faces when he interrupted them. So Rob went to look at the UFO all by himself. Painted on its side it had:

UFO NO. 36

Its door opened, and the owner climbed out. He was made of shining green glass, but his glass face was polite and good-natured.

"Hullo," said Rob. "I'm Rob Stokes."

"I'm Captain Plover," said the UFO captain. "Could you tell me the way to the university, please? I have to collect a friend of mine.

Someone thought he was a rare plant, and took him there."

"I'll show you where it is," said Rob. "Do you want to park your UFO in our garage?"

"It's quite all right, thank you," said Captain Plover. He pushed a button and the spacecraft vanished. Rob hoped he'd be able to find it again. "I would be most grateful if you showed me the way," Captain Plover said. "My friend Cuff keeps sending cross telepathy messages. He doesn't like being a rare plant at a university."

Rob led Captain Plover out into Hollingsworth Road. Captain Plover looked strange with the sun shining through his glass arms and legs, but his boots made a pleasant sound, like lemonade bottles being loaded into a crate on a hot day.

At the milkbar Rob stopped and bought two ice-lollies. Captain Plover said they were delicious. He wasn't stuck up or conceited about being a UFO captain. He didn't show off, and he let Rob wear his glass helmet for a while.

A security guard stopped them at the university entrance. "Children aren't allowed in here on their own," he said.

"Captain Plover's with me," said Rob. "He's not a child."

"Is that Captain Plover?" the guard demanded, and Rob nodded. "You still can't come inside. He's a pretty suspicious-looking character, if you ask me, with that glassy Ned Kelly gear."

He shut the gate in their faces.

"We'll find another way in," Rob said. They

followed some students through a different door.

"Only university staff and students are allowed in here," a girl said.

Captain Plover stepped forward and held out a green glass hand. "I'm delighted to meet you, madam," he said politely, but the girl just stared at him and walked on.

"Never mind, Captain Plover," Rob whispered. "We'll find the plant laboratory by ourselves." So they strode in boldly, following the signs to the Science Department.

Captain Plover's friend Cuff was in a sealed plastic tank in the middle of the plant laboratory, sulking. He didn't look anything like Captain Plover. He was the same size and shape as a cabbage, and each leaf had an eye in its centre. All those little eyes looked very annoyed.

"What took you so long, Plover?" he demanded. "And who's that weird-looking alien you've got with you?"

"It's Rob," Captain Plover explained patiently. "He kindly offered to show me the way here. Without him I would have taken much longer. Rob, would you carry Cuff back to the spaceship? He's not constructed for walking."

Cuff wasn't very grateful for Rob's help. He complained about being bumped up and down all the way along Hollingsworth Road, and he asked irritably why everyone was staring. People certainly were staring. They gazed at Captain Plover with the light streaming through him. They gazed at Cuff's dozens of little cross eyes. And they stared at Rob carrying him.

"It's cleverly done."

"It must be some sort of telly advertisement."

"It's creepy what they can do with plastics and fibreglass," people said.

"Don't take any notice," whispered Rob. "They're silly if they can't tell you're the crew of a spaceship."

"This is a very jerky, boring journey," grumbled Cuff.

"We're there now," said Rob. His dad was cleaning the car.

"Rob, how many times must I tell you not to play with glass?" he said absently.

Rob's Mum was pegging out the washing.

"Put that old cabbage on the compost heap, please dear," she said.

Rob could tell by the way all Cuff's eyes snapped shut and opened again, glaring, that he

clink clink

was very offended. He carried him quickly over the fence to the invisible UFO. Captain Plover pressed the button and the spacecraft re-appeared.

"That was the worst trip I ever had any-where!" Cuff said crabbily as Rob rolled him through the door.

"Don't mind Cuff," Captain Plover said. "He likes everyone to think he's fierce, but he's not really."

He climbed up the steps. Rob was very sorry he had to leave, and he felt in his jeans pocket. "Here's a goodbye present for you and Mr Cuff," he said.

"I don't want a present," Cuff snapped. "Presents are nothing but a nuisance. What would I do with a present, eh?"

But Captain Plover was delighted with the present, which was one of Rob's best things. It was a little canoe carved from balsa wood and painted with Indian designs. Captain Plover put it into one of his glass pockets. Then he pulled out a glass medal, and passed it to Rob. One side had a picture of Cuff, and the other had a picture of Captain Plover.

"Goodbye, Rob," said Captain Plover and he saluted and shut the door.

Rob watched the UFO vanish through a hole in the sky. He went inside and showed everyone the medal.

"It has pictures of the UFO crew," he said.

"It's just ordinary glass," jeered his sister.

"It's just a green magnifying glass or something," scoffed his brother. "I can't see any pictures."

In the kitchen Rob examined the medal, and it looked like a television screen not tuned in properly.

"Hullo, Captain Plover," he whispered. Captain Plover's face appeared in focus, smiled at him and said, "Hello, Rob."

Rob turned the medal over and said respectfully, "Hullo, Mr Cuff." And a picture of Cuff appeared and said ungraciously, "I've got better things to do than waste time chatting every five minutes."

"Come and have lunch, Rob," called his mother. "You can play with that thing, whatever it is, later."

The seance

"A SEANCE WILL BE great fun," said the five guests. (Some of them didn't really think so, but Annabel Chadwick was loud and bossy and usually got her own way in everything.) Annabel cut the letters of the alphabet from a newspaper, stuck them round the coffee table, and put a sherry glass in the middle.

"My Mum says seances are rubbish," Danielle said. "It's just the people round the table moving the glass."

"That might be so in your house," said Annabel. "But it'll be the real thing at *my* seance. I knew as soon as we came to live here that things have happened in this house."

"Nothing's ever happened here. I've lived in this street all my life, and first the boring Dexters owned this house, and after that the Jacksons, and all they did was breed silky-haired terriers and then they moved to Wollongong. And then you came here to live."

Annabel glared. "I meant before the Jacksons and the Dexters," she said. "Some very weird things happened in this house once. I can tell because I'm psychic. You don't know anything about being psychic, Danielle. Now, everyone get in a circle round the table and I'll start the seance."

"First, can I go home and get my pillow?" said Roslyn, who lived down the street. "I forgot it, and I'll never be able to get to sleep later without my own pillow."

"People can't just run in and out of seances. It upsets the ghosts," said Annabel sternly. She lit a candle and turned out the ceiling light. Everyone grew rather quiet. Outside the window there were tree ferns, which cast strange shadows over the pale walls of the living room.

"Put your fingertips on the glass like me," said Annabel. "And then I'll ask *her* to come."

"*Her?*"

"If you're all too scared, we can turn the light on again and play some babyish little game such as Scrabble." No one made the first move to switch on the light. "Noelle and Trudy, if you can't stop fidgeting, you'll have to go and watch black-and-white television with my Mum in the bedroom," Annabel said tyrannically, and Noelle and Trudy stopped fidgeting. "Is there anybody there?" Annabel asked into the darkened room.

The glass moved slowly in a wide arc and touched the little slip of paper that said YES. Roslyn gave a slight yelp.

"What is your name?" Annabel asked. The glass slipped around the polished table and touched various letters. "NAHHAN LISLIW," it said.

"NAHHAN LISLIW?" said Danielle, and giggled.

"It can't spell very well," said Glenys.

"Hannah Willis," said Annabel. "That's what it's trying to say."

The girls rearranged the letters in their minds and fell silent. Rosalyn took her fingertips rather hastily off the glass. "Who's Hannah Willis?" she asked.

"I've made contact with her before," said Annabel. "Poor Hannah Willis. She died right here in this house. Tragically."

"But there was only the Jacksons and their silky-haired terriers and before that those boring Dexters . . ."

"I'm talking about *before* any of us were born. Do you want me to go on with this seance or not?"

"I'll just slip home and get my pillow," said Roslyn, but Annabel looked at her and Roslyn shut up.

"What do you want of the people in this house, Hannah Willis?" asked Annabel.

"I wish you hadn't asked it that," Glenys said nervously. The glass crept from letter to letter.

"CELINGI," said the glass. "GLENICIC. INLECIG. CLING . . ."

"CLING?" whispered Noelle.

"CEILING," said Annabel knowledgeably, and everyone glanced up and rather wished they hadn't. The tree ferns outside spread a menacing spiderweb pattern across the white ceiling.

"If you look very carefully, you'll see there's a profile of a face up there by the light fitting," said Annabel.

Everyone peered through the patterns of moonlight-etched ferns and deciphered what could have been the faint outline of a head in profile. It moved as the fronds stirred in the wind. It seemed to be looking straight down into their upturned faces.

"Let's watch the late movie instead," said Trudy.

"Let's play Scrabble," said Glenys.

"I really have to go home and get my pillow now," said Roslyn.

"There's nothing to be scared of," said Annabel patronizingly. "It's only Hannah Willis come back to visit her house."

"It's only a pattern made by the ferns," scoffed Danielle, but she didn't sound very sure.

"Who's running this seance? Anyhow, that's not the only sign of Hannah Willis's presence in this house. There are other things that happen."

"What?"

"Things get moved. Vases. You put them one end of the mantelpiece, and next morning you find them down the other. And besides, Hannah Willis doesn't always stay up there on the ceiling."

Nobody said anything. They glanced over their shoulders into the dark recesses of the room.

"Once I was lying on the couch with my eyes shut," said Annabel. "And I felt someone pulling my hair . . ."

Noelle hurriedly got off the couch and sat on the floor close to Danielle.

"So I opened my eyes, and there was this old lady in an apron, and she was bending down pulling at my hair. You could see the furniture through her arms and her apron."

"There are no such things as ghosts," said Danielle.

"You weren't here when that old lady ghost pulled my hair, smarty. Anyhow, I've seen her a whole lot of other times, too. Sometimes she sits in the rocking chair, the very one Trudy's sitting in now. You can see the wickerwork through her transparent apron and her poor old transparent hands."

Trudy shot out of the rocking chair and sat on the other side of Danielle. Annabel glanced from face to scared face and felt pleased. She liked being the centre of attention.

"Sometimes I've heard Hannah Willis's poor old feet shuffling along the veranda," she said. "Maybe it'll happen tonight. Sometimes she raps at the veranda door, too, wanting to get back into her house, I expect."

"Why would she knock at the back door?" Danielle demanded. "You made out she just comes and goes as she likes."

"I suppose she uses the back door because she doesn't want to step over the faded old bloodstains by the front door," Annabel said crushingly. "You wouldn't want to be stepping over the spot where you were murdered, either."

"There's no bloodstains by your front door, only an African violet in a brass pot."

"Mum put that there as camouflage. It's not something you spread around, that someone was murdered in your house, even if it was fifty years ago."

"How did you find out, then? You only

moved in eight weeks ago."

"I found out by asking seance questions. I often chat to poor old Hannah Willis when there's nothing much on TV. Like this: Hannah Willis, are you going to come down off the ceiling and walk around the veranda later on tonight?"

YES, said the sherry glass.

"We could always move the party to my house," Roslyn offered.

"I'm the boss of this party," said Annabel huffily. "I'm the one who fixed up the party food and the guest list and everything . . ."

"We didn't know you'd be asking Hannah Willis to it," said Roslyn miserably. "I wouldn't have come if I'd known she was coming."

Behind her in the darkness, the empty rocking chair creaked and began to move.

Everyone, except Annabel, jumped up on the coffee table and screamed.

"Do you want me to send Hannah Willis away, then?" said Annabel, yawning. "I suppose I'd better, seeing you're all so scared." She stood up and spread her arms theatrically and addressed the quietly rocking chair. "Hannah Willis, return to the grave," she ordered bossily. "You're frightening everyone in this room. Except *me*, of course."

The chair stopped rocking and Annabel switched on the light and blew out the candle. "I guess it's time to go to bed now," she said.

"I don't think I'll bother going over to my house in the dark to get my pillow," said Roslyn in a small voice. "I'll just roll up my tracksuit top and use that."

"I'll lend you one of our pillows," said Annabel. But before she went to fetch it, she secretly got rid of the long thread of black cotton attached to the rocking chair. She offered to be the one who had to sleep on the floor nearest to the veranda door. Nobody else offered to. Nobody wanted to switch off the light, either.

"Dear me, how very juvenile," scoffed Annabel, switching it off herself.

Everyone tried to go to sleep, wishing very much that they hadn't come to beastly Annabel Chadwick's beastly slumber party. They lay and listened to the silence of the house.

The silence made it very easy, half an hour later, to hear the slow careful footsteps walking across the veranda, and the something that tapped softly on the veranda door. Everyone shot like starter pistols down to the bottom of their sleeping bags.

The knocking sounded again, tentative, even apologetic.

"Annabel Chadwick, you'll *have* to get up and answer it!" said Danielle. "Tell Hannah

Willis to go away!"

"Please, Annabel!" begged Roslyn, and sounded as though she would start to cry.

"You're the only one here who's psychic, Annabel," said Trudy. "You'll have to go and tell her. You aren't scared, are you?"

"Course I'm not scared," said Annabel, but took rather a long time to get out of her sleeping bag.

"Hurry up!" Noelle pleaded, but Annabel took quite a long time to cross to the veranda door.

"Tell her we won't touch a single thing in her house, or sit in the rocking chair," whispered Glenys.

"You aren't too scared to open the door, are you, Annabel?" asked Danielle.

"Course not," said Annabel, but took a very long time to turn the handle. She opened the door a crack and peered out.

"Annabel?" an old voice whispered out of the shadows on the veranda. "Are you Annabel Chadwick? I've come to . . ."

"No! I'm *not* Annabel Chadwick! Go away!" squealed Annabel, and slammed the door shut on the old woman who stood outside, with her apron shining as clear and white as bone. Annabel fled across the living room and dived into her sleeping bag and wriggled frantically underneath the couch.

". . . I've come to bring Roslyn her pillow. She can't get to sleep without it," finished Roslyn's grandma in astonishment to the slammed door, thinking what bad manners some children had. She left the pillow by the door and went away, stepping slowly and cautiously across the dark veranda.

"Thought you weren't scared of ghosts, Annabel?" everyone whispered indignantly, but Annabel Chadwick didn't say one more word.

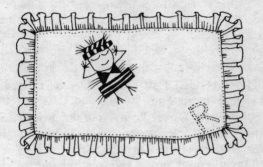

Sitting next to William

THE TROUBLE WITH Oliver was that he was very depressing.

"Get up, Oliver," his mother would say cheerfully. "The sun is shining, and you can wear your new jeans to school."

Oliver would look at the weather and frown. "It may look sunny," he would say, "but so far this year, forty-seven sunny days had a cool change in the afternoon, with thunderclouds developing, and gales causing widespread damage. And if I wore new clothes they'd only get tomato sauce from someone's pie spilled on them."

"I'll pack you a nice lunch," his mother would say.

"Food is bad for your teeth," Oliver would say.

That was how Oliver carried on all the time. The library books he borrowed had such titles as *The Lost Dog* or *A History of Shipwrecks*. He always carried an umbrella in case it rained, and sticking plaster in case he fell over. At school nobody wanted to sit next to him because it was like sitting next to a glacier or a blizzard.

One day a new kid called William started at Oliver's school and he had to sit next to Oliver.

"This desk is in a direct draught," Oliver told him immediately.

They had to illustrate what they had been learning about gold-mining. Everyone drew pictures of people rushing around with nuggets, and balloons coming out of their mouths saying, "Wheeee! Look what I found!"

But Oliver drew a sorrowful man trudging down a road, with NO LUCK printed under it. Then he looked at William's work. William had drawn a whole page of figures lying flat on the ground. "What are they supposed to be doing?" Oliver asked.

"They all died from fever," William said triumphantly, and Oliver felt annoyed.

"I have to have a tooth out tomorrow," Oliver said. "I fell over and knocked it loose."

"That's nothing," said William. "Last holidays I had to have my appendix out. All our bags were packed ready to leave for Sydney, too."

"I always get sick on planes," said Oliver irritably.

"I always get car-sick just going round the block, even if they give me special tablets," William said. Oliver said nothing.

At lunch the teacher told Oliver to show William around the playground.

"We can't play football because I've got nylon socks on today," Oliver said. He waited for William to comment, but William just stood dolefully under a wet tree, letting the drips fall on him. "I'm allergic to nylon," Oliver said loudly. "I'd get blisters if I played football in nylon socks."

William didn't look impressed. "What's so great about being allergic to nylon?" he demanded. "I'm allergic to wool. There's not very many people allergic to wool, I can tell you. I'm allergic to grass, too. That's why I won't be going in any school sports. Anyhow, sports are a waste of time. They only make you feel tired."

Oliver went to get a drink and William followed, though Oliver was beginning to wish he didn't have to look after him.

"I never drink unboiled water," William said. "It's full of bacteria. And you can get stomach-ache from drinking water when you're hot. I reckon it's better to be on the safe side, and only drink water in the winter. And boil it first."

Oliver wished afternoon school would start.

"What's that up on the school roof?" William asked.

"A solar heating system," Oliver said.

"Then it's dumb," William said. "Everyone knows the sun is getting colder and colder."

"Not for millions of years, it won't," Oliver said. "There's plenty of heat left in the sun. I reckon that a solar heater's a good idea." He had never even thought about the solar heater particularly. But he was getting fed up with William capping every remark with another bigger and gloomier.

"The solar heating thing's a waste of time," William said firmly. "Because the world's going to end on Sunday morning. I worked it out on my brother's calculator."

Oliver decided that William was so weird and gloomy that he really might have powers to work out the date the world would end. And Oliver was suddenly aware that he didn't want the world to end. Not ever. He realized that there were some nice things in it, and tried to list some. It was difficult, because he was so used to thinking about cheerless things. Then he remembered how pleasant it was to sit in the living room at home and watch the rain through the window. There were red curtains in the living room. Oliver decided that red was all right, as far as colours went, and he added that to his list. "No one really knows when the world's going to end," he said.

"They didn't till I worked it out on my brother's calculator," William said smugly. "Half-past seven on Sunday morning. I'm not going to bother doing any homework. Anyhow, it's quite a good thing, really. No more worrying about stepping on a blue-ringed octopus at the beach — only I never go to the beach in case there might be a blue-ringed octopus there."

Oliver was so irritated that he moved away, but he yelled over his shoulder, "Hey, William! Standing next to you is like standing next to a glacier or a blizzard!" But then he remembered that he'd been told to look after William and help him settle into the new school, so he groaned and turned back. "Hey, William," he said. "The world's not coming to an end on Sunday. Because Sunday is my birthday, and my Mum has made a cake already! So there!"

"What's so special about birthdays?" William asked gloomily.

"Well," said Oliver, "when the world doesn't come to an end on Sunday, and you're hanging around feeling stupid because it didn't, you can come over to my place for my birthday, if you like."

William looked surprised. "That's funny,"

he said. "No one ever asked me to a birthday party before, though I can't think why."

Oliver started to say, "It's because you're so depressing!" but then he remembered that no one had ever asked *him* to a birthday party either, or wanted to come to his, although his mother had given him some invitations to hand out. He handed one to William. "Don't wear woollen socks on Sunday, and I won't wear nylon ones, and maybe we can kick a football when we finish the cake," he said.

"We can't in your back garden. I'm allergic to grass," William said. He was looking and looking at the birthday invitation, and when the bell rang for the end of lunch-time he said, "But

I'm not allergic to concrete. We could play on the footpath."

And Oliver noticed that he didn't say one more thing about the world coming to an end.

The room
with five doors

JOSIE, WHO WAS TEN, had to share a room with Carla, who was thirteen, and she didn't like it. She wrote this list and gave it to her mother:

WHY I SHOULD HAVE A ROOM OF MY OWN
1 I have no privacy.
2 My mobile keeps falling down and I found a pair of wire cutters under Carla's pillow.
3 Every night she tells this creepy serial about a ghost called Aubrey Clooney who walks round with his head under his arm and he haunts a different house in this street every month and Carla says soon Aubrey Clooney will get round to haunting OUR house.
4 I WANT MY OWN ROOM!

"There's only the old laundry," Mrs Sullivan said. "But it's hardly bigger than a shoebox. That's why your father built me the new one out on the veranda."

But Josie moved into the old laundry that very evening. It had five doors, which led into the kitchen, living room, hallway, bathroom and back veranda. There was just enough space for Josie's bed. It was absolutely fantastic having your own room, she thought blissfully, hanging her mobile from the light fitting. She'd cut out pictures of ballerinas and suspended them from a wire coat-hanger. It was as though all those little paper ballerinas were spinning gracefully specially for her in her very own room.

It was terrific having your own room, she thought, turning off her light and nestling down for sleep.

Her bed shook on its castors. Shane had come home from Youth Club and was using the veranda door. He climbed over her and into the kitchen, and made three sandwiches with cheese and spring onion filling blended in the food processor, and a chocolate thickshake mixed up in the milkshake maker. He had second helpings of everything.

Josie listened to all that electrical gadgetry whirring and thumping, and wished Shane wasn't so greedy, but at last the kitchen was quiet.

But the bathroom wasn't. Her Dad was in there, with the shower on full blast. When he had a shower, he always pretended he was a famous singer. He sang "Some Enchanted Evening", "The Road to Mandalay" and a whole lot of excerpts from Gilbert and Sullivan. Josie thought his singing was really horrible, like the sort of noise a bilious dugong might make. She banged on the wall, but her Dad thought she was tapping out admiring messages in Morse code, so he sang all the verses of "Click Go the Shears" as a special encore.

He finally turned the shower off, and Josie wriggled the frown from her forehead, but she'd forgotten that he always rode the exercise bike in the bathroom for ten minutes after a shower — and that it needed oiling!

At last the whole house was quiet and she lay in bed in her new room and looked up at the ballerina mobile. The new ceiling had weird shadows on it, and the little ballerinas, she suddenly thought, looked as though they were suspended by their necks from a coat-hanger-shaped gibbet.

"Can I ask Rhonda home from school to see my bedroom?" Josie asked in the morning.

"To see your laundry, you mean," Carla said, smirking.

Josie gave her a haughty look and made her bed beautifully in honour of having her own room. It was the first time in her life she'd made her bed without having to be threatened, arrested or court martialled, and her mother choked on a slice of Marmite-on-toast in astonishment.

After school Josie brought Rhonda home and proudly showed off her new room.

"I guess it's handy having an electric wall dryer in your bedroom," Rhonda said doubtfully.

"The dryer's going to be moved out to the new laundry on the veranda," Josie said. "Then I'll be allowed to decorate this room any way I like. I thought of having black and purple walls."

"It wouldn't really matter what colour you painted the walls," Rhonda said. "There's so little of them it doesn't matter. They're all doors."

"The doors make this room nice and airy," Josie said crossly. "When there's a heat wave, I'll have instant cross-current air conditioning."

She served afternoon tea sitting on the bed, but there was a great deal of traffic. Shane came back from Rollerama with three of his mates, Chook, Dobbsy and Slugger. They all skated over Josie's bed and rolled into the kitchen. Mrs Sullivan stepped over Josie's bed and through the door into the bathroom. At least she apologized for interrupting. Carla came through from the hall, heading towards the laundry veranda with her wet bathers, and dripped chlorine water over the afternoon tea.

"You got our biscuits wet," Josie shouted after her.

"You can always dry them off in your wall dryer," Rhonda said.

"This room's nice," Josie insisted. "It has more atmosphere and personality than Carla's room."

"And more doors, too," Rhonda said, her voice creamy as toffee.

That night, while Josie tried to get to sleep, all five doors seemed to be opened and shut as often as a bank door on Friday afternoon just before a long weekend.

And when her Dad finished his shower, he absentmindedly opened the door into the old laundry and tossed in a soggy great heap of wet towels. Josie indignantly crammed them all into the clothes dryer. Then she lay in bed in the five-doored room, thinking how terrific it wasn't.

Sharing a room with Carla, she thought grudgingly, hadn't really been all that bad. Carla often got up and made delightful midnight popcorn using a secret recipe she'd invented which was called Soya Sauce Popcorn à Garlic. And her presence, even when she slept, was comfortable.

Josie looked up at the ceiling with its sinister speckled shadows, and the ballerinas hanging in their nooses, and got up and yanked the mobile down.

People sometimes put ticking clocks in with puppies in strange surroundings. It was supposed to calm them. Maybe she could get up and hunt for a clock. But the clocks in her house were all electric ones. And besides, what if an inexplicable bulky shadow passed in between the little glowing red digital eye and yourself while you were trying to get to sleep?

She looked nervously at the five doors. In horror films, the scariest part was always when a door creaked stealthily open behind an unsuspecting victim. Well, now she was in a room with FIVE doors, and any of them could creak open at any moment. In fact, one murderer could have five choices, or five murderers could creep in and get her all at the same time.

She looked around at her terrific new room, and told herself hollowly that it was just great, it was absolutely marvellous!

Wasn't it?

Josie glared at every door in turn, then dived under the bedclothes and didn't come up till morning.

In the morning she presented her mother with a list.

WHY I SHOULD BE ALLOWED TO MOVE BACK WITH CARLA

1 I have no privacy.
2 Rhonda Zeigler doesn't have a clothes dryer on her bedroom wall, and people don't skate

over her bed when she's trying to sleep, either.

3 People run in and out of this old laundry all night as though it's a 24-hour shop.

4 The light fitting here isn't strong enough for my mobile.

5 Last night in the shower Dad played "Blue Moon" on the saxophone right through seven times, and he hasn't even got a saxophone and can't play it either.

6 I WANT MY OLD ROOM BACK.

PS And I don't get to hear Carla's serial about Aubrey Clooney the ghost who carries his head under his arm, and Carla was getting to a really exciting bit and I want to know what happens!

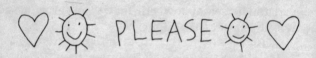

The last pirate

MUDWATER, THE COOK, was the first of the crew to hand in his notice. He didn't know how to write and just scribbled some marks on a bit of torn sail, and Captain Gnash didn't know how to read, but he realized it was a letter of resignation. "I'm leaving, and that's that," Mudwater said. "Piracy is a dying trade and there's just no future in it."

Captain Gnash was so insulted he ran to shove the plank out with his own hands and teach Mudwater a lesson, but the *Saucy Nancy* wasn't a very well run ship, and the bosun was using the plank as an ironing-board. By the time the Captain had snatched it away from him, gibbering with rage, Mudwater and his luggage were safely in the ship's dinghy, out of reach.

"What other treacherous dog isn't happy aboard the *Saucy Nancy?*" Captain Gnash demanded.

Gorilla, the bosun, tied his newly-ironed scarf round his head and stepped forward with his suitcase already packed. "There's a lot of truth in what Mudwater said, Cap'n. I think it's time we all tried to get ourselves jobs ashore," he said. "There's just no call for pirates these days."

"Get off my ship!" yelled the Captain, and Mudwater obligingly rowed back and collected Gorilla, Whiplash, Snake Eyes, Strike Me Dead, and even Coyote the cabin boy. Captain Gnash was left to manage the ship all by himself.

He wasn't very good at it, and after six dithery months the *Saucy Nancy* finally ran aground in a little bay. She settled down cosily like a hen, and dropped her raggedy sails and refused to budge.

Captain Gnash said a lot of very rude words and stamped up and down the decks, and then he finished off the last of his rum and counted up his money. There wasn't much left. "You mind the ship, Bloodred," he ordered. Bloodred was his parrot, but he wasn't very cheerful company. He spent most of his time huddled up with his head under his wing, brooding, and when he wasn't doing that, he was cussing in a mixture of Spanish-Portuguese-Hindustani.

The Captain marched into the nearest town, glaring at everyone who stared at him, and went into a bottle-shop to buy some rum. When the attendant told him the price, Captain Gnash grabbed him up by the collar and shook him like a tablecloth. "You thieving octopus!" he roared. "Try to cheat a man over the price of rum, would you? Take that and that!" He whipped off his pirate hat and buffeted the man over the ears. The man called the manager and complained.

"What seems to be the trouble?" asked the

manager politely. Captain Gnash cried out in disbelief, "Thunder and lightning! It's Mudwater!"

"Hush," said Mudwater, looking around nervously. "I'm not called that any more. I changed my name to Henri, and I've got this nice little restaurant and bottle-shop business."

"Mudwater, why don't you come back to the ship eh?" coaxed Captain Gnash. "It's hopeless, being a pirate on my own."

"I don't want to be a pirate any more," said Mudwater. "Anyhow, I never did like cooking at sea, with everything tasting like seawater and jellyfish. Now I've done a course in gourmet cooking."

"Bah!" said the Captain. "What's wrong with a few weevils in biscuits? I'm disappointed in you, Mudwater. Here, hand over some rum, and I'll be off."

"I'm afraid rum doesn't come in kegs any more," said Mudwater.

Captain Gnash had only enough money to buy a tiny little gift bottle of rum, the size of a perfume bottle. He was too ashamed to be seen carrying something like that in public, so he stuck it under his hat and went back to the ship, muttering and grumbling about how rotten things had become.

"There's only one thing to do," thought Captain Gnash gloomily. "And that's advertise for more crew and start all over again."

He put the advertisement in the local paper and waited, but there were only two replies. The first person was a frail, elderly retired gentleman who was president of the local model railway and toy yacht hobby club. "Stop wasting my time!" Captain Gnash bellowed and chased him ashore with a belaying pin.

A boy leaving school saw the advertisement and came down with his mother, and she wasn't at all impressed with the *Saucy Nancy* or Captain Gnash. "I wouldn't let my Jonathan go to sea on an awful-looking leaky old boat like this!" she said.

"Ship!" yelled Captain Gnash. "The *Saucy Nancy*'s not a boat, drat it!"

"And just look at the dust over everything! Don't you ever vacuum the floor?"

"Decks!" Captain Gnash said sourly. "They're called decks."

"And I'm certainly not having my Jonathan run up and down those ricketty-looking post things!"

"Rigging!" cried Captain Gnash. "Masts and rigging!"

"Come along home, Jonathan," said the lady firmly.

After they left, Captain Gnash hunted around the galley for something to eat. There wasn't any food left at all, not even parrot seed, and Bloodred made a terrible fuss in Spanish-Portuguese-Hindustani. "All right!" said Captain Gnash. "Quit nagging me, you old feather duster! I'll just have to get a job of some kind, that's all."

He counted up the things he could do: patch sails, jump from one bouncy ship to another on a high sea without losing his balance, sword-fight, and swear. None of these things seemed to fit any career he could think of, except being a pirate, and that was all finished. It seemed very sad, and a tear rolled down his cheek and melted in his whiskers. But he realized that he would have to find some other job, just to survive, and that would be that—the end of the last pirate.

Next morning he buckled on his sword and set Bloodred on his shoulder and marched up to the top deck and saluted the skull-and-cross-bones flag for the last time before taking it down.

"Hold it!" someone called from the beach. "A little more to the left, please! Perfect!"

Down on the beach there was a van with a large camera mounted on it, and people measuring out distances, and people writing things down on clipboards. Captain Gnash didn't care for strangers to be peering at his ship and writing things down that he couldn't read, and he let out a bellow that whipped a cloud of sand from the dunes and blasted the circling seagulls five metres higher in the air.

"What a fantastic vocal range!" said the person in charge. "I think we could do without amplifiers."

Captain Gnash rattled his sword loudly along the deck rails, which made a noise like a kid running a stick along a fence. He got out the plank and dusted it off in full view and meaning-fully set it over the side of the ship, but even that didn't send the strangers on their way. It seemed to encourage them.

The man who was in charge climbed aboard without being asked. Captain Gnash glared at him, and almost wished that he'd had the chance to take him on as cabin boy. He would soon have taught him not to wear embroidered muslin shirts and wear his hair all curled up and blonde-tipped like a girl.

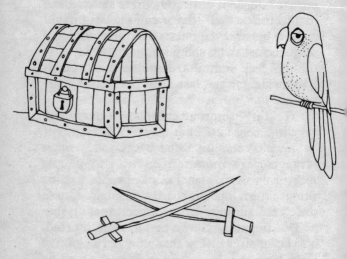

"I'm David Fairweather from the channel eight television network," said the young man. "We've been looking for a location for a new advertising series."

"Get off my ship or I'll tip a bucket of swill over your head!" said Captain Gnash in a not very friendly manner.

"Wonderful!" said David Fairweather, writing furiously. "What a marvellous stroke of luck finding you!" He dashed around looking at things and making notes.

"Oy!" said Captain Gnash. "Get your hands off that there brass lantern!" But David Fairweather had finished admiring that, and was in the captain's cabin, inspecting the carved oak panelling. Captain Gnash was livid. He never let anyone enter his cabin because he always kept a deck of cards spread out in a very complicated game of patience that never worked out. He'd been playing it for forty years, ever since he first went to sea, and it hadn't ever worked out once, not even when he cheated, which was every time. And now here was this David Fairweather, a sissy name if ever he heard one, calmly pushing the cards aside and spreading out a big pile of documents and a new-fangled pen which wasn't even made from a bird's plume.

"This is the contract," he said. "We can start filming right away, because you certainly won't need any acting lessons. You're a complete natural. And that's why I'm offering you the job."

"What do you mean, acting job?" demanded Captain Gnash. "I've a mind to cut off your ears and feed them to my parrot! Offering me an acting job indeed! What an insult!"

David Fairweather read out aloud the part in the contract which said how much money he'd be earning, and the Captain felt less insulted.

"Thunder!" he said, impressed. "But no one's getting me up on any stage," he added. "I'd never be able to look Bloodred in the eye again."

"It wouldn't be on a stage. We'd film the advertisements here on your ship."

"Advertisements?" roared Captain Gnash. "After-shave lotion and sissy things like that? No one's getting me to shave off my whiskers, when it took me forty years to grow them! Get off my ship!" He chased David Fairweather briskly up on deck at the tip of his cutlass and dumped him over the side.

"It's not for after-shave lotion," David Fair-weather said, picking himself up and dusting off his elegant pants. "It's for rum-flavoured toffee."

"And don't come back, either!" hollered Captain Gnash, and then he stopped. "What flavoured toffee?" he asked. "What's that you said, young feller?"

"Rum. Here try one. They're very good toffees, you know. A new brand."

Captain Gnash removed the wrapping and popped the rum-flavoured toffee in his mouth and tasted it. It was rich and dark and creamy and delicious. He hadn't tasted old-fashioned rum like that for years, not since the good old days when being a pirate had been a flourishing trade. "You mean I'd get paid for eating these?" he asked. "And I wouldn't have to leave the *Saucy Nancy*?"

"That's right. It's a good contract. You'd be foolish to turn it down, and if you don't mind my saying so, Captain, there's not much future in being a pirate these days."

But Captain Gnash still had enough pirate spirit left in him to demand that a separate contract be drawn up for Bloodred, too, before he signed anything. Bloodred appeared in every one of the commercials, perched on Captain Gnash's shoulder and leering evilly at the camera. He added comments of his own in Spanish-Portuguese-Hindustani, but nobody could understand them, which was probably just as well.

Anti-snore machine

MARTINE KIRBY WAS good-natured and generous. Also, her father owned a chocolate factory, so when it was time for the school camp, everyone wanted to be in her room. In fact so many people wanted to that Miss Lewis, the teacher in charge of the camp, finally had to draw lots. Tracey, Paula and Bronwyn won. Tracey and Paula were extremely pleased, but not about having to share with Bronwyn, who was Tracey's little sister.

Everyone had terrific fun that first night, doing all the usual things such as filling each other's shower caps with talcum powder, and fighting over who was going to have the only top bunk. "I don't mind not having it," Martine said generously. "I sleep like a log, anyhow, no matter where I am."

So Paula and Tracey felt ashamed of being greedy, and let her have the top bunk. (Also, they remembered about the midnight feast and her Dad owning a chocolate factory.)

"Showers, PJs and lights out at ten," Miss Lewis said. "Anyone talking after that will have to sleep in the creek with the bunyips."

But the midnight feast went on much longer. Martine shared all the sweets her Dad had given her with everyone along the corridor. All that glucose gave everyone a tremendous surge of renewed energy, and Miss Lewis stopped calling out indulgently, "Girls, put the lights out now, please." She yelled instead "LIGHTS OUT THIS MINUTE STOP THAT TALKING AND I WON'T SAY IT ONE MORE TIME!" So everyone knew she meant it and shovelled the chocolate wrappers off their beds and got ready to go to sleep.

Martine Kirby didn't have any trouble at all. She blinked once or twice at the ceiling, shut her eyes and fell asleep instantly.

And snored.

It wasn't ordinary snoring. It could best be described as a combination of a hippopotamus with sinus trouble, an electric sander, a truck dumping a load of gravel, peak-hour traffic along a six-lane motorway and a dam bursting its banks.

Everyone sat up in bed saying polite things such as, "I say, Martine, do you mind . . ." and "Martine, excuse me, but do you realize . . . ." But none of that had any effect and they started to bellow at her instead. They all had their hands clapped over their ears to block out the sound of Martine snoring, and didn't realize how loudly they were yelling until Miss Lewis opened the door, glaring.

She wasn't very sympathetic. "You'll just have to get used to it," she said crossly. "One person snoring shouldn't keep everyone else awake. Put some cotton wool in your ears."

So they tried cotton wool, plus shredded tissues and the hoods of their sleeping bags over that, but nothing could blot out the sound of Martine Kirby's snoring. She kept it up all night, not missing one single beat. In the morning she bounced out of bed, glowing with health and rest, all ready for a brisk five-kilometre run before breakfast. No one else in that room looked rested. They all had tired red eyes and weary expressions.

"We couldn't get any sleep all night because of your snoring!" Tracey and Paula said.

"I didn't know I was snoring," Martine said apologetically. "I always sleep so soundly. Though come to think of it, maybe that's the reason why my sister Angela moved out of our room and into the garage. But I'll try not to snore tonight. I promise."

Promises are all very well.

That next night, Martine put on an astonishing performance, as though the previous night's snoring had just been a practice run. You might as well have tried to get to sleep in a cathedral belfry with all the bell-ringers and their understudies practising Christmas carols.

"We can't go a whole week without sleep," Tracey said desperately.

"We could try—" Bronwyn said shyly, but she was frowned at for daring to speak.

"I'll just have to invent a special machine that cures snoring," said Paula, who came from a long line of engineers. Seeing that it was useless to think about sleep while Martine was not only thinking about it but doing it successfully enough for a whole army, Tracey sat on Paula's bed and watched her design a snoring machine on a sheet of paper.

"It looks very complicated," Tracey said doubtfully. "And it's going to be hard to get all those things in the middle of the night."

"Why couldn't we—" said Bronwyn, but Paula and Tracey hit her with a pillow and told her to mind her own business.

"This is how my machine works," said Paula. "I'll stickytape a paper bag, open end down, on the wall just above Martine's face. Above the bag there'll be a sheet of cardboard. Fixed to that will be a glove stuffed with something heavy, like a boxing glove. Above the glove will be another board, and poised on one end will be a heavy object, such as a desert boot. Just below the desert boot, on Martine's bedside table, there's a ruler balanced over a matchbox, and on the other end of the ruler, there's a bowl of water. And in the bowl of water the thickest, soggiest sponge we can find."

"Much easier to—" said Bronwyn, but Paula and Tracey turned round and looked at her as though she were some kind of worm.

"Martine's snoring will inflate the paper bag," said Paula. "The bag of breath will push against the cardboard. The cardboard will push up the glove which will punch the board holding the heavy object. The heavy object will fall on to the ruler edge which will tip the saucer of water and the sponge right in to the middle of Martine Kirby's snoring and make her shut up!"

"Wow!" said Tracey, but Bronwyn didn't say anything. She just looked as though she didn't think that machine would work. But Paula and Tracey made her go out into the dark corridor and into the craft room and search around till she found all the things necessary for Paula's invention. It would have been hard to find her way back to their room in the dark, but Martine's snoring served as a very good beacon.

Paula built the machine, and when it was finished, she and Tracey looked at it with

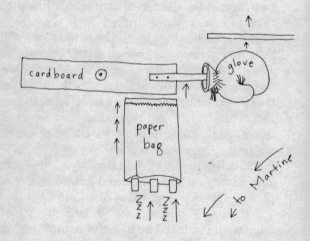

admiration. Paula even took a flashlight picture
of it for her files.

"I don't think it will work," Bronwyn said,
but no one took any notice of her at all.

It was as though Martine knew, even in her
sleep, that some momentous experiment was
taking place, for her snoring grew even louder
than the previous night. Very slowly the paper
bag above her face began to swell. It billowed

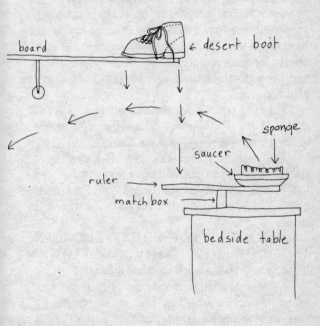

like a balloon and pushed against the cardboard shelf. The glove, stuffed with chocolate papers and socks, moved, too. It rapped the board above, and the carefully balanced desert boot slipped off, as clean as an anchor. The desert boot crashed down on the ruler edge. The saucer of water and the sponge jumped into the air and landed with a loud wet splosh right in Martine Kirby's face.

"ZZZZZZZZZZZ ZZZZZZZZZZZZZ," she said, without even flickering an eyelash.

Paula burst into tears of disappointment, thwarted genius and sheer exhaustion from having no sleep for two nights running. Tracey tried to comfort her, but it's hard to murmur soothing words against a background of trumpeting snores.

"I'll ring up my Mum and get her to come and pick me up," Paula said, sniffing. "I'm not going to miss a whole week's sleep."

"Me neither," said Tracey. "Is there room for my things in your Mum's car?"

"I don't want to go home yet and miss camp," Bronwyn said. "Anyhow, I think I can—"

"WHO TOLD YOU YOU COULD JOIN IN GROWN-UP CONVERSATION!" Tracey and Paula both said indignantly.

"—stop Martine's snoring," Bronwyn finished. She stood on her bed and very gently turned Martine Kirby off her back and on to her side.

"There," Bronwyn said into the sudden calm of the snoreless room. "That's how you stop people snoring."

Brother Ninian's blot

BROTHER NINIAN WRIGGLED his blue toes energetically inside his sandals. Brother Melchior on the next stool, completing a beautiful fifth page of Latin manuscript, didn't wriggle at all. He sat with his back as straight as a tombstone.

Ninian looked gloomily down at his own work. Twice he'd written *Donime nom sun digmus*, getting the Ns and Ms mixed up; there was an inky thumb-print in the left margin and a whole missed line that he'd desperately and unsuccessfully tried to squeeze in later. The whole page was a mess, and he couldn't really blame it on the poor light down his end of the desk. (It was very strange, he though suddenly, how Brother Melchior, in spite of being so saintly, always managed to get that good seat by the window.)

Brother Melchior certainly appeared to be sneaking sideways glances at his terrible work now. Although he was so holy, Ninian could sense what he was thinking, as though a bubble floated above his tonsure with printed Latin words inside saying, "You dunce, Ninian! Just look at that good bit of parchment all ruined! Things will change if *I'm* ever made Abbot, just you see, my lad!''

Ninian felt depressed. Soon Father Cuthbert would be around to collect the completed pages. Perhaps he'd even be sent out in disgrace to work in the kitchen gardens. He didn't want to. He was always getting his herbs muddled and coming back to the refectory with a bunch of onionweed when he'd been sent to gather mint and rosemary. And although it was cold in the library, it was a great deal colder out in the kitchen gardens.

He hastily smoothed out a fresh sheet of parchment, praying that this time he wouldn't make any mistakes. He worked hard, not even stopping to warm his cold fingers around the candle, or furtively tuck his blue feet up inside the hem of his robe for warmth. He toiled with tremendous effort until he'd finished a new copy of the ruined sheet.

There, all done! Not one muddled M or N, not one blot, and all the lines more or less even, except for the last, but if you kept your head at an angle, it didn't look all that peculiar. Maybe Father Cuthbert would even praise him! Usually when he came to collect the morning's work, there would be an ominous silence, then a hiss of outrage, followed by a lecture about wasting parchment and threats about being sent back to work in the kitchen gardens.

But not this time, Ninian thought cheerfully. He would have liked to nudge Brother Melchior and perhaps boast a little, but monks weren't allowed to show off. Brother Melchior certainly never did, though come to think of it, he did have a way of spreading all his immaculate finished manuscript sheets over the desk instead of stacking them in a pile. But that was probably just to air them or something. It was unthinkable that someone as holy as Brother Melchior would ever show off! So Ninian resisted an urge to jab him in the ribs with the handle of a quill pen and yell into the hushed shadows of the library. "Hey! Look at this neat page I just did!" To start with, he didn't know how you said that in Latin, and Brother Melchior never spoke anything else.

He allowed himself a few seconds of gazing blissfully at his completed page. Not one mistake! Brother Melchior stopped writing, rather pointedly, though that was an uncharitable thought—he was more likely praying.

Ninian reached guiltily for parchment to begin another page of good work, but his hands, clumsy with cold, knocked over a rack of quills. The rack nudged the pot of ink and it tipped over. Ninian watched, horrified, as a fat dollop of ink plopped like a deathwatch beetle on to the top left-hand margin of his laborious, error-free work.

The blot didn't stay put. It rolled gently down the length of the page, following the slope of the desk, and then stopped. But before running out of ink, it forked into three, like the root of a tree. His beautiful page was ruined!

Brother Melchior had seen, though he didn't say one word. He just stared with his pale eyes. "Brother, are you going to cop it!" that stare said, just as surely as though sung in plainchant.

But that was another sinful thought; Brother
Melchior was much too holy to gloat.

Ninian rubbed with his sleeve at the blot, but
managed only to smudge it. The smudge didn't
improve things. He tried to disguise it with a lot
of little feathery strokes, as though he was just
testing the point of his pen, and because the
whole thing looked so much like a tree, his quill
started to doodle leaf shapes.

Actually, drawing dozens of tiny detailed
leaves took his mind off Brother Melchior's
silent disapproval, and Father Cuthbert's expected disapproval, which certainly would *not*
be silent at all. The blot had quite an interesting
shape if you looked at it closely, a bit like an oak
tree. Ivy grew on old oaks. Ninian drew ivy
twining about the trunk and then trailed the ivy
across the lower edge of the page and half-way
up the right margin. But now the top looked a
bit bare.

He drew a chubby cloud sailing over the tree
top. It looked bare, too. Something should be
sitting on that cloud. An angel! He liked angels.
So he drew one sitting on the cloud and gave it a
kind, motherly face, the sort of face that belonged above a pudding basin and mixing
spoon. But he gave this one a magnificent
trumpet that curled across the top margin to
meet the ivy growing up the other side.

It was much more fun, really, than printing
letter after patient, tedious Latin letter.

Flowers, he thought, would look pretty
amongst all that ivy; arum lilies and daisies—
and a small hare crouched in between them. He
didn't make the hare scared-looking, for after

all, there was an angel up above the tree top, not a hawk. As he worked, he could almost imagine that he himself could hear the angel's trumpet music tootling softly and cheerfully all around the arches of the library, and wouldn't that give Brother Melchior a surprise! Brother Melchior!

He realized suddenly that there was no longer the sound of a quill scraping across parchment from the next stool. There was only the sound of silence, a rather terrifying one. Brother Melchior was just sitting, watching, and behind him stood Father Cuthbert, tall as a steeple, also watching.

Both of them were staring at his page of Latin, disgracefully littered all over with the flowers trees hares ivy clouds angels trumpets and O, my goodness, he'd even drawn a monk on his knees saying an *Ave* amongst all that clover! The monk was thin and bony and obviously had trouble with rheumatics, and Ninian saw to his horror that he'd given that monk Father Cuthbert's face! O, Brother, was he going to cop it!

And Brother Melchior was clearly hanging around just to hear him get into trouble. Surely he'd put away and taken out that long eagle quill four times already?

Ninian didn't feel cold any more; even his toenails were red with embarrassment. Father Cuthbert leaned forward and picked up the sheet of parchment delicately in his long white fingers. He took it over to the window for a better look. Ninian made himself as small and inconspicuous as possible inside his brown robe. He pulled up the hood, and folded his hands into the sleeves to hide their trembling.

Wilfully spoiling expensive parchment! he thought desperately. And drawing rabbits on the same page as angels and Latin prayers, and a caterpillar, and—("O, Blessed Saint Gideon, my patron saint, please come to my assistance in a hurry, Sir!")—drawing a picture of the *Abbot* himself, only much fatter than he really was, actually holding a dandelion and blowing away the seeds like a child playing clocks!

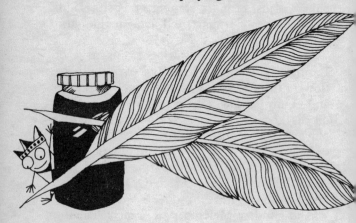

He hadn't even realized he'd put *that* in until Father Cuthbert spread the dreadful sheet out on the window sill. The sun streamed in upon it, bright and crisp and clear. ("Saint Gideon, couldn't you have arranged for a nice handy eclipse just now?" Ninian thought, rather crossly.)

And he knew for certain that Brother Melchior was surely hanging around to hear him being told off! The kitchen gardens for sure, Ninian thought in anguish, and three hours on my knees in chapel, and O, how bitterly cold it is in there!

He peeped out from under his hood. There was something odd about all this silence. But Father Cuthbert's face didn't look angry at all. It was filled with respect.

"What a splendid idea, to decorate the margins in such a beautiful manner!" he said. "Truly inspired! Brother Ninian, from now on, you may decorate all the pages thus, and our abbey will have the most wonderful books in the world. Brother Melchior can do all the printing and leave you free to concentrate upon this new and amazing idea."

"It would look even better with touches of

colour," Ninian dared to suggest humbly.

"And so it would! I'll arrange for some to be brought to the library this afternoon."

"Gold paint would look nice too," said Ninian meekly.

"Brilliant! There is some gold leaf left over from gilding the cherubs on the chapel ceiling. I'll fetch it. I don't wish to interfere with your creative talent, but do you think you could possibly add a gold halo to this saintly-looking monk on his knees praying amongst the clover?"

"Of course, Father Cuthbert," Ninian said. "No trouble at all."

"Very well done, my son."

My son! Usually he avoided calling Ninian that, if possible.

"You'd better swap stools with Brother Melchior and be by the window," Father Cuthbert said. "We can't have you straining your eyes at such important work. And we must arrange for heating. Brother Melchior, pop down to the kitchen and fetch some logs for a fire. Can't have a fine artist like young Ninian risking chilblains on the fingers, can we?"

Brother Melchior obeyed instantly, so saintly, obedient and holy was he.

Ninian blinked.

For as Brother Melchior passed him, he could almost have sworn, by his patron saint, too, that a jealous tongue was stuck out at him from beneath that hood. Accompanied by some very rude whispered words, not one of them in Latin!

Irritating Irma

IRMA WAS VERY good at climbing. Her parents were calm people, who, if they saw Irma clamber up a church steeple or the outside of a lighthouse, would just murmur admiringly, "Lovely, darling." So when they took a holiday cottage near some steep cliffs and Irma told them she was going looking for eagles, they just said, "Lovely, darling."

Irma began to climb the cliffs and half-way up she found a little door. The door belonged to a dragon who was having a very nice long sleep, and he wasn't a bit pleased to be woken up. He stared at Irma's teeth braces and glasses and he wasn't very impressed. He rumbled like a forge.

"What a cute green lizard!" said Irma.

The dragon, insulted, uttered a huge echoey roar which splintered granite flakes from his cave.

"That's a nasty cough you've got," said Irma.

The dragon eyed her Spiderman T-shirt and torn jeans and the cap that she had got free from a petrol station. He remembered clearly that maidens usually wore dear little gold crowns and embroidered slippers, and they always squealed when they met him and looked ill at ease. He glared at Irma and spurted forth a long, smoky orange flame.

"No wonder you've got a cough," Irma said. "Smoking's a nasty habit and bad for your health. And this cave certainly is musty and it needs airing."

The dragon made a noise like bacon rashers frying, but Irma was busy inspecting everything. "You need a broom for a start," she said. "And maybe a cuckoo clock up there by the door. Tch! Just look at the dust over everything! Tomorrow I'll bring some cleaning equipment and anything else I can think of."

When she left, the dragon set to work, only he didn't do any dusting. He collected boulders and filled up the cave entrance. Bouldered up, and fortressed up, and buttressed up, he smiled grimly to himself and went back to sleep.

Some hours later he woke to a whirring headachey rumbling. Granite chips rattled around his ears, and Irma scrambled in, carrying a bright pneumatic power drill. "Good morning," she called. "There must have been a landslide during the night. But I cleaned it up."

The dragon's scales rattled. Angry little flames flickered in his jaw. He made a noise like a hundred barbecues and he squinted ferociously at Irma.

"Don't frown like that," she ordered, tying on an apron. "You'll end up with ugly worry lines. There's a lot of work to get through this morning. First I'll sweep this gritty sand away, and you could really do with a nice carpet in here, or maybe tiles would be better. If there's one thing I just can't stand, it's disorder."

The dragon sizzled fretfully, but worse was to come. When Irma finished tidying up, she turned her attention to him. She bossily trimmed and lacquered his claws. She polished his scales and lifted up his wings and dusted under them with talcum powder. The dragon blushed but Irma didn't take any notice, because she was busy tying a blue ribbon around his tail. "I've got to be going now," she said. "But I'll be back tomorrow."

The dragon watched her climb down the cliff. "There's only one way to get any peace," he thought. "I'll just have to eat her. Tomorrow. Freckles will taste nasty, and so will ginger hair, but maybe if I shut my eyes and gulp, it won't be so bad." He groaned. Parents, he knew from past experience, usually came looking for devoured maidens, waving lances and acting very unfriendly.

When Irma arrived next morning, he opened his jaws, without much enthusiasm, ready to eat her, but Irma said, "Look what I brought you!"

She shoved a plate under his nose. On it was a layer cake with strawberry cream filling, iced with chocolate icing, sprinkled with hundreds and thousands, lollies, whipped cream and meringues. The dragon shuddered weakly and felt ill.

"You look as though you're coming down with the flu," said Irma. She took his temperature and spread a blanket over him. The blanket was fluffily pink and edged with satin binding, and the dragon thought it was very babyish. Irma wrapped it around him and fastened it with a kitten brooch. "I'll leave you to get some rest now, you poor old thing," she said.

"You will?" thought the dragon hopefully.

"But I'll drop by first thing tomorrow," said Irma. "It's lucky for you I still have three weeks of my holiday left."

And for three weeks, every day, she came, and the dragon suffered. She decorated his cave with pot plants and cushions, a beanbag chair, posters, a bookcase, calendars, and a dart board, and she brought along a toothbrush and bullied him into cleaning his teeth.

But at last, one morning she said, "I've got to go back to school tomorrow. You'll just have to look after yourself till next summer holidays."

When Irma left, the dragon purred and capered about the cave. "Hooray!" he thought. "Good riddance! No more boring chatter and no more being organized, and best of all, undisturbed sleep!" He curled up and shut his eyes.

But his dreams were fretful, and he got up at day-break feeling tetchy and cross. He paced his cave and wondered why the silence seemed weary, and the hours bleak and long. He brooded and nibbled at a claw, and crouched in his doorway staring down at the beach, but it was empty, because all the holiday people had gone. Irma had gone.

"Hooray!" he roared. "And she won't be back for many glorious months!"

But why, he wondered glumly, were tears rolling down his cheeks?

Everywhere he looked in his cave he saw things Irma had lugged up the cliff to decorate his cave without permission. "Yuk," said the dragon morosely, and he kicked a pot plant over the cliff. A wave snatched at it, and the dragon gave a roar of anger and slithered down the cliff and grabbed it back. He carried it crossly back to his cave and plonked it down on Irma's bookcase.

"Even when she's not here, she's irritating," he thought. "I should have eaten her and got it over with. And the very next time I see her, irritating Irma will be my next meal! Freckles and all! Just wait!"

And he waited, but all his little flames flickered out one by one, and his scales lost their sparkle, and his ribboned tail drooped listlessly.

Winter howled through his cave, and he brooded, and led a horrid, bad-tempered life.

But at last gay umbrellas began to blossom like flowers along the beach, and it was summer. The dragon sharpened his teeth against the rocks and tried to work up an appetite. And the day came when Irma bounced in through his door, and the indignant dragon opened his massive jaws wide.

"Hello!" cried Irma. "I meant to write, but I forgot your address, but just look what I brought you! Suntan lotion, and a yo-yo with a long string so it will reach down to the bottom of the cliff, and a kite with a picture of you on it, and now tell me, did you miss me? I certainly missed *you*!"

The dragon blinked in despair at her tangly

plaits and glasses and teeth braces. "She's talkative and tedious and her manners are terrible!" he reminded himself fiercely.

("And yet," he thought, "it's strange, but I rather like her face.")

"Nonsense!" he roared to himself. "She's annoying and bossy and an utter little nuisance, and no one invited her here; she just walks in as though she owns this whole cliff!"

("And yet," he thought, "of all the maidens all forlorn, I rather like her best.")

"Didn't you miss me?" demanded Irma.

The dragon began to shake his head indignantly, but try as he could to prevent it, the headshake turned into a nod.

"Then we'll celebrate," said Irma. "What would you like for lunch?"

"Plain scones, please, Irma," said the dragon.

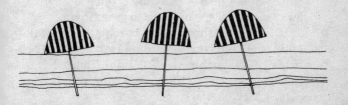

Swapcard season

IT WAS REALLY Vikki's fault that the town got into such a mess. One day she was sorting through her hundred and five swapcards. Her mother stopped ironing and picked up one particular swapcard. "What a lovely picture of a chinchilla cat," she said. "I'd like to have it to make into a bookmark."

Vicki wasn't usually selfish, but that chinchilla cat was one she would never part with. She grabbed it back and said, "No, I'd never give away that one in a million years! I've had it since kindergarten. Anyhow, you don't give away swapcards. You have to swap them."

Vikki's mother wasn't usually hasty-tempered, but she was tired from doing the ironing. She snapped, "All right, then! Keep that old swapcard! I'll go and buy myself one just like it!"

She stopped doing the ironing and went up to the newspaper shop. They had very nice swapcards. Mrs Brown looked for one just like the one Vikki wouldn't part with. At first she just searched for cat ones, but they had so many delightful swapcards of everything in the world that she forgot about being sensible and bought forty assorted ones. Furthermore, she didn't go home and finish the ironing. She called in to show them to a neighbour.

"Oh, they're so pretty," Mrs Webb said. "I wish you'd give me that nice one with the fishing-boat on it. I always wanted to be a sailor."

"You don't give swapcards away," said Mrs Brown. "You have to swap them."

Mrs Webb became quite interested, and she went up to the newsagency and bought every single card they had with ship pictures on them. She showed them to the postman.

"Why, I have hundreds of swapcards at home," said the postman. "I used to collect them when I was a boy. I'll just run home and see if I can find them. Don't swap that oil-tanker one, Mrs Webb. Save it for me." He hurried home and crammed his mailbag with swapcards. Every house he delivered letters to, he knocked on the door and asked if they were interested in swapcards. It was remarkable how many people had collections put away somewhere.

And that's how it started. That's how the whole town got into a mess. All the grown-ups became crazy about swapcards.

The policeman on traffic duty signalled drivers to pull over to the kerb, but not because they had done anything wrong. He had his helmet filled with swapcards, and he kept asking people if they had pairs to this one or that one.

Everyone was very late for work. But it didn't

matter, because when they arrived at work, they

didn't do any. They were too busy showing other people the new cards they had bought or swapped the day before and arranging their collections in various orders of colour or sets.

The great swapcard mania swept right through town. There were long queues of grown-up people outside shops waiting to buy matching pairs to their favourite card. Some parents were even sneakily raiding their own children's swapcard collections by torchlight in the middle of the night, just to get three of a kind.

People started to stay home from dental appointments. With their tongues poking out of the corners of their mouths in concentration, they would put the swapcards lovingly in their albums. It didn't really matter, because the dentist had closed his surgery while he drilled holes in all his five thousand and seventy-three swapcards. He was turning his waiting-room into a swapcard art gallery.

The only sensible person in the whole town was the school principal, Mr Jasen. He hadn't gone crazy about swapcards because he had spent too many years having to confiscate them from children who swapped them at assembly when they should have been paying attention.

"This has got to stop," said Mr Jasen. "None of my teachers is teaching any more. They're all sitting in the staff-room drinking coffee and swapping cards. Who started this in the first place, anyhow?"

Everyone turned around and looked at Vikki. She guiltily put up her hand, although she didn't want to, because Mr Jasen looked so cross. "It was my mum who started it," she confessed, "But it was me who started my mum."

"Well, then," Mr Jasen said sternly. "You had better think of a way to end all this nonsense. I couldn't get any milk for my cornflakes this morning. The milkman has gone off to the city to hunt for cards with pictures of Clydesdale horses on them."

Vikki went home glumly. She knew it wasn't any use offering her mother the chinchilla cat swapcard that had started the fuss in the first place. It was too late. By now her mother had forty-three chinchilla cats, as well as all the hundreds of other cards that filled every shelf and empty shoebox in the house, and even the dog kennel.

Vikki went into her driveway. Her mother was swapping cards over the side fence with the lady next door. "You can have this pair of pixies doing knitting on mushrooms, if you give me that orange one of the huntsman spider . . ."

"But I'd rather have the dinosaur with the ribbon round its neck. Or some Olde Worlde cottages if you have any. And they have to have golden edges. I'm going in for gold edges now. They're fashionable."

Vikki suddenly remembered that her mother liked to be fashionable. Her mother was always the first in the street to see a new film or wear a new hairstyle and everyone always copied her because she looked so smart. Vikki smiled to herself.

"Vikki," said her mother. "I'm sorry, but we're having rissoles again tonight. I haven't had time to make anything else. I've been all over town finding someone with the green Viking. Now I have the whole set. Come here and look."

"I don't want to look," said Vikki airily. "No one's bothering about swapcards anymore. It's

yo-yo season!"

She pulled her yo-yo out of her jeans pocket and did some complicated things with it.

Next morning at school Mr Jasen asked if she had done anything about the matter of the swapcards. "Oh yes," said Vikki. "I think you'll find it's all under control now. There weren't any grown-ups swapping swapcards as I came to school. Not in our street."

"That's more like it," said Mr Jasen. "I hope the nonsense will stop now."

"Yes, Mr Jasen," said Vikki humbly, but she didn't tell him that all the grown-ups she had passed that morning in her street were standing at their front gates showing off yo-yo tricks with nice new yo-yos.

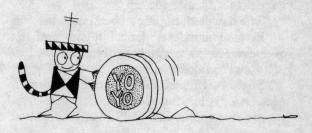

Jane's mansion

JANE LIKED PRETENDING to be grander than she really was. One day she was walking home from school with a new girl named Kylie, and was showing off as usual.

"We have five Siamese cats at our house. And a special iced lemonade tap."

Kylie dawdled, hoping to be invited in.

"I'd ask you in," said Jane, "but my mother's overseas. She's a famous opera singer."

"Wow!" said Kylie.

"She's singing in Paris. Our housekeeper, Mrs Grid, is looking after me. Our house has twenty-five rooms full of Persian carpets and antique furniture."

Kylie looked at Jane's house, thinking that a house containing such splendours would somehow look different.

"Don't take any notice of the front view," said Jane. "My Dad built it like that to trick burglars. Inside it's different. My father is a millionaire."

She waved goodbye airily and went inside.

The house certainly was different inside!

The living room was carpeted with gorgeous

rugs, and had a silver fountain labelled "iced lemonade". The cane furniture had been replaced by carved oak.

"*Mum!* Did we win a lottery?" Jane yelled excitedly. Her mother wasn't home, but a note had been left in the kitchen. It read:

FROM PARIS GOING TO MILAN TO SING TOSCA, AFTER THAT VIENNA. HOUSEKEEPER WILL LOOK AFTER YOU, LOVE, MUM.

Jane read the note and then phoned the factory where her Dad worked. A voice said, "Sorry, it's not possible to speak to Mr Lawson. He's overseas inspecting all his oil wells, diamond mines and banks."

It was Jane's turn to say Wow!

She went into her room to change. Normally her room was a clutter of dropped clothes, unmade bed, and overdue library books. But now it was magnificent. Jane was so impressed that she hung up her school dress instead of letting it lie like a gingham puddle on the floor.

She ran all around the splendid house looking at everything. It was amazing that such a vast mansion could fit into an ordinary suburban block. The back yard was too stupendous to be called that. There was an in-ground pool in a huge lawn. She couldn't even find the fences that separated her house from the neighbours.

"Not that I'd want to, now I'm a millionaire's daughter," she thought smugly.

At six a brass gong summoned her for dinner at a long table lit by a candelabrum. There was one place set. "Don't put your elbows on the table, Miss Jane," somebody strict said. It was Mrs Grid, the housekeeper, and she was just as impressive as the house.

Jane couldn't even resist showing off to her. "I've got to go to the Youth Club," she said when she had finished dinner. "I won every single trophy. It's Presentation Night."

"I'll have Norton bring the car round to the front door," Mrs Grid said.

Jane waited by the front steps. A huge car drove up, and a uniformed man held the door open for her. Jane remembered telling Kylie that she had a chauffeur. She felt very important being driven to the Youth Club like that. Everyone's parents had come for Presentation Night. She regretted that hers were overseas, specially when the club president announced, "Trophy for the most advanced member —Jane Lawson".

No sooner had Jane received the trophy and sat down than the president said, "Cup awarded for callisthenics—Jane Lawson", and she had to go back. She won every single prize, but it wasn't nearly as nice as she thought it would be. After her tenth trip to the stage, the clapping sounded forced, and most of the parents were glaring at her.

When she got home she showed the trophies to Mrs Grid.

Mrs Grid only said, "All that silver will take a

lot of polishing. I've already got enough to do looking after this mansion."

Next morning her father cabled that he was in Brazil buying coffee plantations. Jane rang Kylie to brag.

"My Dad bought me a pair of skates," Kylie said excitedly. "Want to come round and see?"

"Skates are nothing," Jane scoffed. "My father bought *me* a *horse*."

There was a loud neighing at the window, and she put the phone back and went to look. A large horse was trotting around the garden. "Put your horse back in his stable at once," Mrs Grid said crossly.

"I don't want to," said Jane, but Mrs Grid looked at her so sternly that she lied quickly, "We have a groom to look after my horse."

A bandy-legged man in jodphurs appeared and led the horse away. Jane was relieved, because she was really scared of horses.

She went for another walk around her mansion, finding a whole lot of things she'd lied into existence in past conversations with people. There was a trained circus poodle, a crystal bathtub with goldfish swimming round the sides, a real little theatre complete with spotlights, a gymnasium in the basement, and five Siamese cats. She had a marvellous time playing with all that, but she was starting to feel lonely. Mrs Grid was too busy and crotchety to be company. Jane rang Kylie again.

"Come round and I'll let you ride my horse," she offered.

"You wouldn't come round to see my skates," Kylie pointed out, offended.

"We've got a real theatre and a crystal bath with goldfish swimming round the sides. Come round to my house and play," Jane begged.

"I'd better not," said Kylie.

"Why not?"

"Your house sounds too grand. I'd be scared of breaking something valuable. I'd better just play with you at school." She hung up.

Jane sat and looked at all her trophies, and tried to feel proud. But she knew very well she hadn't really won any of those glittering things. She'd only got them by lying.

She missed her parents dreadfully, and remembered that this weekend her Dad had intended to make her a tree house. But he was in Brazil instead. "Where's my shell collection and my pig I made out of a lemon?" she asked Mrs Grid, starting to cry.

"I threw all that rubbish out," said Mrs Grid.

"And there's no point moping. Your parents have to work very hard to keep you in the manner you prefer. You'll just have to wait till Christmas to see them. I daresay they'll be able to drop in for a few minutes then."

"I'm getting my own speedboat for Christmas," Jane boasted, lying automatically through her tears.

"That reminds me," said Mrs Grid. "This telegram arrived for you."

STATE MODEL AND COLOUR PREFERENCE FOR SPEEDBOAT WILL HAVE DELIVERED DEC. 25 LOVE ABSENT PARENTS.

Jane bawled louder.

"Just as well you're going away to boarding school tomorrow," Mrs Grid said. "So I won't have to put up with that awful noise."

Jane was shocked into silence. She remembered lying to the neighbours that she'd won a scholarship to boarding school. She didn't want to go. She wanted her own house to be the way it usually was, with her own nice comfortable parents in it.

"You could pack your things for boarding school now," said Mrs Grid. "I'll get Norton to drive you there early."

Jane jumped up. She ran out of the house and down the street to Kylie's. When Kylie opened the door, Jane babbled feverishly, "We don't have a swimming pool, lemonade tap, horse, groom, miniature theatre or five Siamese cats, and I'm not going to boarding school. My Dad's not a millionaire, he's a fitter and turner. And my Mum can't sing for toffee. We haven't got any antiques or Persian carpets, and I didn't win any trophies at Youth Club. I'll never tell any more lies ever again! And we haven't got a housekeeper, or a chauffeur called Norton. Please come up to my house to play, Kylie."

"All right," said Kylie. "I knew you were lying anyhow."

They went back to Jane's house, and Jane drew a big breath and opened the door. It opened into her usual living room with its old cane furniture, and she could hear her Mum in the kitchen, singing off-key. Jane ran and hugged her. "Where's Dad?" she asked anxiously.

"Just gone up to get the timber for your tree house," said her mother. "You can take some scones into your room if you like."

"My room hasn't got a four-poster bed or a TV set in the ceiling," Jane said to Kylie before she opened the door.

"I didn't think it had," said Kylie.

They ate their scones while they looked at Jane's shell collection and the pig she had made out of a lemon. The scones tasted much nicer than Mrs Grid's cooking. "We haven't got a gymnasium in the basement or a poodle or a speedboat either," said Jane. "I tell a lot of lies."

Her mother came to collect the scone plate.

She was cross about something.

"Who stripped the enamel off the bath tub and put goldfish in the sides?" she demanded.

J. Roodie

J. ROODIE WAS wild and bad, although he was only nine. Nobody owned him, so he lived in a creek bed with his animals, who had nasty names. His dog was called Grip, which was what it did to passers-by. He had a bad-tempered brumby called Kick, and a raggedy crow called Pincher. Pincher swooped down and stole kids' twenty pence worth of chips when they came out of the fish and chip shop. J. Roodie had trained him to do that.

Nobody ever went for a stroll along the creek, because they knew better. J. Roodie kept a supply of dried cow manure and used it as ammunition, because he didn't have pleasant manners at all. He never had a bath and his fingernails were a disgrace and a shame.

There was a cottage near the creek with a FOR SALE notice, but no one wanted to live near J. Roodie. Everyone muttered, "Someone should do something about that awful J. Roodie!" but nobody knew what to do and they were too scared to get close enough to do it, anyhow.

J. Roodie painted creek mud scars across his

face, and blacked out his front teeth. He drew biro tattoos over his back and he stuck a metal ring with a piece missing through his nose so that it looked pierced. He swaggered around town and pulled faces at babies in prams and made them bawl, and he filled the kindergarten sandpit with quicksand. Luckily the teacher discovered it before she lost any pupils.

He let Grip scare everyone they met, and he let Kick eat people's prize roses, and he was just as much a nuisance going out of town as he was going in. But nobody came and told him off, because they were all nervous of tough J. Roodie and his wild animals.

One day he was annoyed to see that the FOR SALE notice had been removed from the cottage and someone had moved in. He sent Grip over to scare them away.

Grip bared his fangs and slobbered like a hungry wolf at the little old lady who had just moved in.

"Oh, what a sweet puppy!" said the little old lady whose name was Miss Daisy Thrimble. Grip had never been called "sweet" before, so he stopped slobbering and wagged his tail. Miss Daisy Thrimble gave him a bath and fluffed up his coat with a hair dryer. "I'll call you Curly," she said. "Here's a nice mat for you, Curly."

Grip felt self-conscious about going back to J. Roodie with his coat all in little ringlets, and besides, the mat was cosier than a creek bed, so he went to sleep.

J. Roodie waited two days for him and then he sent Pincher to the cottage. Miss Daisy was hanging out washing. "Caaaaawwrk!" Pincher croaked horribly, flapping his big, raggedy, untidy wings and snapping his beak.

"What a poor little lost bird," said Miss Daisy. She plucked Pincher out of the sky and carried him inside. She filled a saucer with canary seed and fetched a mirror and a bell. "I'll call you Pretty Boy," she said. "And I'll teach you how to talk."

Pincher already knew some not very nice words that J. Roodie taught him, but Miss Daisy Thrimble looked so sweet-faced and well-behaved that Pincher didn't say them. He tapped the bell with his beak, and looked in the little mirror, and decided that it was very nice to have playthings.

J. Roodie grew tired of waiting for Pincher, and he sent Kick to scare Miss Daisy away. Kick pawed the lawn and carried on like a rodeo and rolled his eyes till the whites showed.

"Oh, what a darling little Shetland pony!" said Miss Daisy. She caught Kick and brushed away the creek mud and plaited his mane into rosettes tied up with red ribbons. "There's a cart in the shed," she said. "You can help me do the shopping. I'll call you Twinkle."

Kick snorted indignantly, but then he saw his reflection in a kitchen window and was amazed that he could look so dignified. He stopped worrying about his new name when Miss Daisy brought him a handful of oats.

J. Roodie marched over to the cottage and yelled, "YAAAAH!" at the top of his voice. He jumped up and down and brandished a spear and rattled some coconuts with faces painted on them, which were tied to his belt. They looked just like shrunken heads. "WHEEEEEE!" yelled J. Roodie. "GRRRRRRR!"

"What a dear little high-spirited boy!" said Miss Daisy. "But you certainly need a bath." She dumped J. Roodie into a tub and when she had finished scrubbing, he was as clean and sweet-smelling as an orange. Miss Daisy dressed him in a blue checked shirt and nice clean pants and brushed his hair. "There," she said. "I shall call you Joe. I'll be proud to take you into town with me in my little cart."

She sat Joe Roodie next to her, and Kick, called Twinkle now, trotted smartly into town, and Grip, called Curly now, ran beside and didn't nip anyone they met.

People said, "Good morning, Miss Daisy. Is that your little nephew?"

"His name is Joe," Miss Daisy said proudly. "I think he lived in the creek bed before he came to stay with me."

"He can't have," they said. "J. Roodie lives in the creek bed and he'd never let anyone else live there."

"J. who?" asked Miss Daisy, because she was rather hard of hearing. "Do you know anyone called J. something or other, Joe?"

Joe Roodie didn't answer right away. He'd just felt in the pockets of his new pants and found a pocket knife with six blades, and a ball of red twine, and some interesting rusty keys, and eleven marbles.

"We'll buy some apples and make a pie for our supper," said Miss Daisy. "Maybe we could invite that J. boy they said lives in the creek. What do you think, Joe?"

Joe Roodie hadn't tasted apple pie for as many years as he hadn't had a bath, and his mouth watered.

"There used to be a kid called J. Roodie in the creek bed," he said. "But he doesn't live there anymore."

How Clara Bebbs put Strettle Street properly on the map

STRETTLE STREET looked like a long boring sentence with no punctuation marks. No one ever moved away, and nobody new ever came there to live. Nothing exciting or different ever happened there, and the postman always knew exactly how long it would take him to get up one side of Strettle Street and down the other side. The footpaths were made of tired grey concrete, which looked dismal even when the sun was shining.

So, Clara Bebbs, who lived at number forty-seven, decided to put Strettle Street properly on the map. She bought a box of silver foil stars and glued them all over the footpath. It took ages, but she had plenty of spare time because it was school holidays.

People walking along Strettle Street and examined the stars glittering beneath their feet. "It's nice, once you get used to it," they said.

There was a very steep hill in Strettle Street. Clara Bebbs noticed that people had difficulty with their heavy shopping trolleys, so she went home and designed an apparatus. She was extremely good at engineering although she was only ten. The apparatus she designed was a wire running along fences, with hooks and a pulley. She showed Mrs Agnew how it worked. "You just attach your shopping trolley to a hook and pull this lever," she explained.

Mrs Agnew did that, and watched her shopping trolley trundle gently up the steep hill to her front gate. "I'll tell the other ladies," she said. "Fancy finding something like that in Strettle Street!"

"Oh, its nothing, really," Clara Bebbs said modestly. "I can think up lots more complicated things."

There was a brick house that had always been empty. It was quite new, but nobody ever bought it because Strettle Street looked such a dull place to live. Clara Bebbs asked the estate agent if she could borrow the house for the school holidays. She made it into a swimming pool by removing the roof and filling all the rooms with water. "It's free," she told everyone in Strettle Street. They liked it very much, because they could wave to their neighbours while they swam about behind the picture windows, and the chimney made a very good diving tower. Even the postman had time to stop for a swim, because he just had to hitch his mailbag on to Clara Bebb's automatic shopping trolley apparatus, and it trundled gently up and down Strettle Street all by itself.

Clara bought some tins of special paint that glowed in the dark and painted all the doors in Strettle Street in beautiful colours. "That's pretty," said the people who lived there, and instead of staying inside watching television in the evenings, they all came outside to look at everyone's front doors instead.

Clara Bebbs built a stage in the middle of the street where it wouldn't interfere with the traffic, and she started evening competition programmes. Every evening she thought up a new, interesting competition, such as who could suck a lemon the longest without pulling a horrible face, and who could touch their ear with their elbow, and who could learn to play the mandolin in ten minutes. The competitions became very popular, and people brought along folding chairs, and their knitting, and their babies in carrybaskets.

In the daylight hours, Clara used the stage for a "Bring Something, Take Something" market. People would arrive with goldfish bowls, and three balls of purple mohair wool, and net bags filled with cumquats, and stuff like that, and they put all the things in a pile on the stage, and you could choose anything from the pile to take home with you.

Next Clara organized brisk, exciting chariot races for Saturday afternoons, with real chariots she built herself in her parents' tool shed. If you didn't like chariots, she had free pachyderm rides, or you could just sit and watch the races from the steel observation tower she built at the end of Strettle Street. On week days she used the tower to instruct people who wished to learn sky diving.

Strettle Street was looking less and less boring. Clara rented some earth-moving equipment, and set to work on the vacant block of land next to her house, and made a marvellous

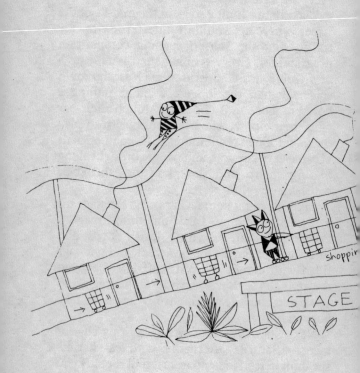

jungle, with monkeys and a swamp and tropical butterflies.

When she finished that, she designed and constructed a huge slippery slide, which swept from one end of the street to the other, suspended above the rooftops. And she also made an underground tunnel beneath Strettle Street,

ending in an underground lake lit by concealed lighting. You could cross the lake using ten-metre high mechanical stilts with inbuilt safety nets, which anyone could use after three minutes' easy practice.

Soon Strettle Street didn't look boring at all, and lots of people who didn't even live there would come along to visit and see what new things Clara Bebbs had designed that week. They told friends, who came also, and Strettle Street became rather too noisy and crowded, in spite of the ten-storey cantilevered car park Clara had built above her parents' tool shed.

"It's not really fair," Mrs Agnew told Clara Bebbs. "We can hardly move with all these new people standing around gaping. Why don't they all go back to their own streets and leave us in peace?"

"Maybe because their streets are just as boring as Strettle Street used to be before I decided to put it properly on the map," said Clara Bebbs. "But I'll think of a solution."

So she added an eleventh storey to the car park, and installed a large electronic sign which said *College for Street Decorators*, and in no time at all she had over a hundred students enrolled for the first lecture. Soon Strettle Street wasn't the only interesting street in town, and crowds ceased to be a problem. All the visiting people were back in their own streets, fixing them up nicely, as Clara Bebbs had shown them in the College for Street Decorators.

When the holidays ended and she had to go back to school herself, everyone who lived in Strettle Street thanked her for her time and trouble. "There's nothing we need now," they said happily. "We've got everything possible in Strettle Street."

"I forgot one thing, though," said Clara Bebbs. "A cat for every front door mat, that's what I forgot."

So she called in at the lost cats' home and

collected forty-seven cats and placed one on each front door mat as she walked up Strettle Street on her way to school.

"There," she said. "Now it's finished."

About the Author

Robin Klein grew up in Kempsey, New South Wales, Australia, with eight brothers and sisters, and a mother who wrote short stories. Her family was very poor and had no books, so Robin wrote her own. She left school at fifteen, and for the next twenty-five years worked at all sorts of jobs including nursing, raising her four children, librarianship, painting and craft.

Robin has been a full-time writer for many years now, with seven novels and over a hundred short stories, poems and plays to her name, including the much-loved *Thing, Penny Pollard's Diary, People Might Hear You* and *The Broomstick Academy*. Her books have won several awards.

Robin lives in bushland in the hills near Melbourne, Australia, with her own creek at the bottom of the garden, and the Puffing Billy steam train within earshot.

HARRIET AND THE HAUNTED SCHOOL

Martin Waddell

ISBN 0 590 70441 9   £1.25

Finding a horse for Anthea to practise sitting on wasn't much of a problem for Harriet. But choosing a place to keep it was. The Games Cupboard provided a cosy home and the horse could take its exercise at night!

But the late-night ghostly hoofbeats terrified the cleaning lady, Ethel Bunch. There was only one solution: the Slow Street Vigilantes and the Anti-Harriet League had to join forces—and set up a phantom trap!

Harriet is back!

THE BROOMSTICK ACADEMY

Robin Klein

ISBN 0590 70575 X   £1.25

The last thing Thalia Birtles wants to do is attend Madame Aquila's Academy for Young Witches! But everyone else in her family is a witch and her mother is determined that she will be too. But all Thalia can see in a crystal ball is her own reflection and she can't even seem to cast a spell!

How can Thalia convince her mother that all she can do with a broomstick is sweep?

GET LAVINIA GOODBODY!

Roger Collinson

ISBN 0 590 70351 X   £1.25

Lavinia Goodbody was a snooty toad—or so her cousin Figgy thought when she came to stay and took over his bedroom.

So Figgy decided to teach Lavinia a lesson and he gave the Gang their orders . . . to GET LAVINIA GOODBODY!

HARRIET AND THE CROCODILES

Martin Waddell

ISBN 0 590 70309 9   £1.00

Harriet spells trouble, for teachers and for everyone else, too. She is very upset when her pet yellow snail disappears but looks forward to selecting a new pet during the class trip to the zoo.

Why is it that only Harriet thinks her crocodile is sweet and charming?

An hilarious story introducing Harriet who is already a firm favourite with 7-9 year olds.